## DOG IN THE DUNGEON

"Aminta came back! She can't be a stray, she just *can't* be. She's here for a reason," Mandy said urgently. "Let's go to the gallery and look at the dog portraits, okay?" Tilly and James nodded eagerly.

"I think I remember the way," James said, as they hurried off up the staircase to the second floor.

"Oh, good," Mandy said, as James's finger on the light switch brought the windowless little gallery to life. They stood clustered at the heavy wooden door, gaping, as a hundred painted eyes gazed back at them from the walls. Mandy looked along the row of portraits until she came to the one of the deerhound with the distinctive white diamond in the middle of her chest.

"There!" cried Mandy. "There she is — there's our Aminta!"

*Read more spooky Animal Ark™ Hauntings tales*

1 Stallion in the Storm
2 Cat in the Crypt
3 Dog in the Dungeon

# Dog in the Dungeon

**Ben M. Baglio**

**Illustrations by Ann Baum**

**Cover illustration by**
**John Butler**

AN
**APPLE**
PAPERBACK

SCHOLASTIC INC.
New York Toronto London Auckland Sydney
Mexico City New Delhi Hong Kong Buenos Aires

ISBN 0-439-34408-5



12 11 10 9 8 7 6 5 2 3 4 5 6/0

Printed in the U.S.A. 40

First Scholastic printing, November 2001

**Special thanks to Ingrid Hoare.**
**Thanks also to C. J. Hall,**
**B. Vet. Med., M.R.C.V.S., for reviewing**
**the veterinary material contained in this book.**

# *One*

"There it is," said Mandy Hope excitedly. "Up on top of the hill."

Dr. Adam, Mandy's dad, flicked on the overhead light and slowed the Animal Ark Land Rover to a stop on the side of the winding road. "Yes, I think you're right," he agreed. "Skelton Castle. Looks a bit spooky, doesn't it?" He looked around and grinned ghoulishly at Mandy and her best friend, James Hunter. Mandy wrinkled her nose at her father.

James cupped his face in his hands, pressing his glasses up against the car window. "It does," he mumbled.

"What an unusual place to live," observed Dr. Emily.

Ahead of them, the castle loomed majestically from a faint swirl of blue evening mist. Two towered gate-houses stood guard on either side of a massive, heavily chained drawbridge.

"It's a real castle," said Mandy. "I thought it might just be a sort of big, fancy house."

"Oh, it's real, all right," Dr. Adam said. "It was built in the thirteenth century, so I'm told, as a fortress, when Skelton Castle would have had a working moat and men mounted up on the battlements."

"Wow," said James.

"Come on, Dad! Let's go." Mandy looked at James with shining eyes.

"Are you sure you want to?" asked Dr. Adam, in a voice that quivered playfully. "We may never live to tell the tale of our weekend in Skelton Castle."

"Don't be silly!" Dr. Emily smiled, digging her husband in the ribs with a well-aimed elbow. "Mr. Blaithwaite sounded charming on the telephone. I'm sure he doesn't eat his guests for breakfast or anything like that. He just has *different* taste when it comes to choosing a new home."

"Well, I'm up for it," James said seriously, moving away from the window and rubbing his eyes. "I can't wait to see inside."

"Okay," Dr. Adam agreed. "But while you and Mandy are having a good time exploring the castle, spare a thought for those of us who are here to earn an honest living."

Mandy's parents ran a veterinary practice called Animal Ark Veterinary Clinic in the Yorkshire village of Welford. Animal Ark had been recommended to Max Blaithwaite by one of his friends. He had called to ask if they could be on hand when he arrived at Skelton Castle with his large collection of pets. "I'm prepared to pay," he had told Dr. Adam cheerfully, "whatever it costs. I'm an old fusspot, I know, but I'm very fond of my animals and it will be a long and arduous journey for them. I want to be sure they've arrived in peak condition."

So Dr. Adam and Dr. Emily had agreed to work at Skelton Castle the weekend that the Blaithwaites and their menagerie moved in.

"It was nice of Mr. Blaithwaite to invite us to stay," James said, looking at Mandy. Mandy nodded.

"Mr. Blaithwaite has a granddaughter who is moving up north with him," Dr. Adam explained. "He thought it might be fun for her to get to know someone around the same age. So he said that you and Mandy were more than welcome."

"And Blackie, of course!" James grinned.

Hearing his name, James's labrador, Blackie, blinked, his eyes glazed from his long doze in the car. He shuffled with some difficulty into a sitting position between Mandy and James on the backseat. Lifting his nose, he sniffed deeply at the open window. The air was heavy with the scents of summer. Dr. Adam turned off the road and through a pair of imposing wrought-iron gates onto a sweep of graveled drive.

The castle stood at the crest of a gently sloping hill. As the Land Rover climbed, Mandy could see the clustered rooftops of a small town in the valley below. They passed along an avenue of trees and entered a wood of huge oaks. It was cool and dim in their shade. Mandy noticed rotted and muddy wagon tracks that led to the thatched, peaked roof of a small house some distance away.

"Look," she said, "over there to the left. It looks like a little cottage. I wonder who lives there?"

"Perhaps nobody. It's a huge estate," Dr. Adam observed. "There could be any number of homes tucked away on the grounds. I suppose it might once have been a gamekeeper's cottage, or a hunting lodge."

The driveway wandered on uphill toward the castle, running alongside a fast-flowing stream that soon disappeared underground, then widened out onto open land. "There's a stable yard over there," James said, pointing at a grassy area enclosed by split-pole fencing.

"Oh," Mandy said. "They must be planning to build something here. Look, Mom, Dad, there are trenches dug into the ground." Dr. Emily looked over to her left.

"It looks like the foundations for something," she said. "Perhaps they're building a wall." Metal stakes pierced the trim lawn at intervals, and a red-and-white rope looped between them to warn people of the yard-wide ditch.

"It's a beautiful castle," Mandy said, as they got closer. "But it looks a little sad to me. It needs cheering up." A tangle of vines and other plants had sprung up in the bed of the empty moat and had reached out to climb and cover the walls of solid gray sandstone. Several of the windows were covered by overgrown vines.

"Look, James, there are arrow-shaped slits cut into the towers!" Mandy said, pointing. James looked. "I hope we can go up there and explore," she added.

The engine of the Land Rover idled while Dr. Adam figured out where to park it. Blackie gave a short bark as an elderly man wearing a blue apron came striding out across the drawbridge of the castle, one hand raised in a salute of greeting. He looked sweaty and exhausted.

"Hello," Dr. Emily called, getting out of the car. "Mr. Blaithwaite?"

"Booth, ma'am," he said. "Mr. Blaithwaite's butler." He gave a polite little bow. "Welcome to you all. Mr. Blaithwaite and his granddaughter are expected here tomorrow morning. I'm to help you settle in."

"It's a butler," James whispered to Mandy. "I mean, *he's* a butler. I didn't think anyone had butlers anymore."

"My wife Ellie and I came a few days ago," Booth explained, shaking hands with Dr. Adam. "The castle was sold to Mr. Blaithwaite with its contents included, and as you can imagine, there's a lot to do to make the place comfortable. If you leave your luggage in the car, we will deal with it later. Please, come with me."

"May I bring my dog, Mr. Booth?" James spoke up.

"Ah, yes, I'd forgotten we have a four-legged houseguest this weekend. How splendid. Give him a quick walk, then bring him into the kitchen. And by the way, call me Booth. I prefer it."

Booth hurried off across the drawbridge and into the castle. After stretching their legs briefly, Mandy, James, and Blackie followed Dr. Emily and Dr. Adam. Their footsteps were loud against the slatted wooden drawbridge, and they had to duck to enter under the portcullis — the heavy grating that once was lowered to block the gateway to the original fortress.

Once inside, they were led along the dimly lit stone-covered passages that led toward the kitchen. Booth stepped briskly ahead. He made so many turns that Mandy lost her sense of direction completely. Blackie's wagging tail thumped expectantly against James's leg as he trotted along in the gloom. Then Booth stood aside at a narrow stone-arched door to the castle kitchen and moved aside to let them pass. They found themselves in a warm, brightly lit room. The contrast was so great that Mandy had to squint to adjust her eyes to the sudden glare. Ellie Booth looked up from a large stove and spread her arms by way of greeting.

"Well, here you are!" she said, as if there had been some doubt they would come. "It's good to see you all. I've got a meal ready and the beds are made up. And *you*, I expect," she said, bending down to Blackie, "will want a bowl of cold water."

"This is Blackie. He's very friendly," said James reassuringly, patting Blackie's silky head. He turned and grinned his approval at Mandy. It was going to be a great weekend. Ellie Booth had a wide smile and a gentle manner and, judging by the mouthwatering smell in the kitchen, she could cook, too.

Blackie, having quenched his thirst, retired comfortably under the large polished wood table and put his nose on his paws with a sigh. "Sit down, please!" Mrs. Booth urged. "I'm sure you would all welcome something to eat and drink."

"Wow, what a feast," James said, as Mrs. Booth set out dish after dish of food.

"It's nice to have someone to cook for," she said, putting a steaming dish of small buttery potatoes under James's nose. "We've only been up here a couple of days, but we're already feeling a little isolated. Oh, the castle is beautiful, but it needs to be brought back to life! Start, please. Just dig in."

There was a platter of cold cuts, a quiche, salads, large hunks of yellow and orange cheese, and a large crusty loaf of bread, still warm from the oven and giving off a wonderful smell. Dessert was a large fruit pie with whipped cream. Mandy avoided the meat without feeling awkward. Mrs. Booth wasn't likely to be bothered by her vegetarianism, she could tell.

"This is delicious. Thank you." Dr. Emily smiled.

"Skelton Castle *is* a very isolated spot," mused Dr. Adam, looking at Mr. Booth. "Why did Mr. Blaithwaite choose it?"

"Mr. Blaithwaite loves history." Booth chuckled. "He's talked of buying a castle ever since I came to work for him as a young man. Now he's got his dream." Booth looked around at the solid old walls approvingly.

"Mr. Blaithwaite's granddaughter is twelve, like me, is that right, Mrs. Booth?" Mandy asked, spearing a slippery potato with her fork.

"She's eleven now, going on twelve. A darling child," Ellie Booth said, smiling. "She'll enjoy having your company for the weekend, I'm sure. And James's," she added.

"Mr. Blaithwaite takes care of Tilly," Booth said, "and is a good parent, too. She's an only child and needs a firm hand at times."

"That's nonsense, Booth," Mrs. Booth responded, chuckling. "Why, Mr. Blaithwaite's a softy and you know it!" Mrs. Booth passed Dr. Emily a slice of quiche.

"All those animals!" grumbled Booth, helping himself to the salad. "He'll have to limit his collection soon or he'll have to turn this place into a zoo!"

"The animals are Mr. Blaithwaite's passion," Ellie Booth explained. "He and Tilly are both crazy about all animals; they collect strays from all over the place."

"Do they have a dog?" James asked.

"Had one — up until a year ago. Her name was Honey. A beautiful collie crossbreed. She was very old when she died and Mr. Blaithwaite was very attached to her. He hasn't wanted a replacement, though Tilly would adore another dog. Perhaps when they've settled here in the castle he'll let her have one."

"They've already got enough animals to be taking care of," Booth grumbled, though Mandy noticed that he was smiling. "Everything from a llama to hamsters."

All those pets! It sounded like heaven to Mandy. She, too, had been passionate about animals for as long as she could remember. She tried to picture Tilly, wondering what she looked like and if they would get along. "I can't wait, can you?" she asked James.

"What for?" James was finishing a last mouthful of pie.

"For tomorrow, of course, when Mr. Blaithwaite and Tilly arrive with their pets. I can't wait to get to know them all."

"Me, too," James said. "I hope she's nice."

"Any tea, Ellie?" asked Booth, wiping his mouth with a large linen napkin.

Mrs. Booth pushed back her chair. "I'll make a pot now," she replied, then looked at Dr. Adam and Dr. Emily. "I expect you would like to see where you're sleeping. And after that, would you like to go and explore?" she said to Mandy and James.

"Yes, please, Mrs. Booth," Mandy said.

James nodded and asked, "Do you want any help cleaning up?"

"How kind of you. But it's no problem, James, thank you. You run along and have a look around. It's a fantastic place."

"Um," James began. "Is it okay if Blackie sleeps with me? That's what he's used to."

"I don't think anyone here will have a problem with that, James." Mrs. Booth smiled.

"I've brought his basket," James added.

"Let's go and get the luggage out of the car, and I'll take you up," Booth suggested.

"Thank you, Mrs. Booth," said Mandy, standing up.

"That was a lovely meal," Dr. Emily said, pushing back her chair.

"It certainly was," Dr. Adam agreed. "All right, lead on, Mr. Booth."

Dr. Emily and Dr. Adam, with Mandy and James, followed Booth back along the stone hallway. Booth helped Dr. Adam with the few bulky bags and James carried Blackie's basket. The labrador trotted along happily, his nose twitching as he took in the intriguing smells of the castle. As they came into the hall, Mandy noticed a huge, carved-marble coat of arms, along with several painted portraits of stern-looking people hung on the walls. She looked at James, who raised his eyebrows. "Pretty impressive," he whispered.

"I believe the Skelton family owned this place for generations," Booth told them, as they began to climb the wide, uncarpeted, elm staircase that led upstairs. "As the family's fortunes declined, parts of the castle had to be closed off. Mr. Blaithwaite plans to use a group of rooms on the upper two floors only — apart from the kitchen, down below."

"Have you and Mrs. Booth explored everywhere?" Mandy asked.

Booth laughed. "There's been no time for that. I expect it will take us a week or so even to *find* all the rooms!"

Booth stopped when he reached a half-landing. "To the left are the main bedrooms. Your rooms are on the right, off that hallway."

A few moments later, Booth flung open a heavy wooden door. "Your room, Dr. Emily and Dr. Adam," he announced, putting down the bags. Blackie barged ahead to investigate.

"Oh, it's beautiful," Mandy exclaimed. The large double bed was a four-poster, and above it was an elaborately plastered ceiling. In the curving bay window was a cushioned window seat. Mandy looked out. The garden stretched out below for as far as she could see.

"All right, now, Mandy and James. If you follow me, I'll show you where you'll both be sleeping, then you can wander around," Booth said. He turned to Dr. Emily. "We'll leave you to settle in, okay?"

"Fine." Dr. Adam smiled. "Take care of yourselves, Mandy and James," he teased in an eerie whisper. "We might see you again, or we might not!"

"Oh, Dad!" Mandy sighed.

"C'mon, boy!" James called to Blackie. Booth led them along the narrow, wooden-floored hallway. "Miss Tilly was given a choice of rooms on this floor," he said. "She chose the one at the end of the hall with a large window in it. Yours are side by side, opposite hers."

"It's like a hotel!" said Mandy. "It's huge!"

"Here we are," Booth said. "I'll put the bags in this one, and you can decide where you'd like to sleep."

"Thanks," said James, putting down Blackie's heavy basket with relief.

A smooth mahogany wood door swung open and Mandy and James peered in. The bedroom was carpeted in red and it, too, had a stone-vaulted window with a wide, cushioned seat. Light slanted in through the cracks in the studded wooden shutters. The ceiling was heavily beamed in the same dark, shiny wood as the floor. Booth unbarred the shutter and folded it back. Soft light streamed in. "This is nice," James said, grinning at Mandy.

Blackie sniffed around, then climbed into his basket

and settled down. Mandy laughed. "It looks like Blackie has decided this will be your room. I'll go next door."

"See you later, then," Booth said. "Will you be able to find your way around?"

"I'm sure we will, thank you." Mandy smiled.

Her room was similar to James's, but it had a washbasin and a pretty mirror and a small stone fireplace, the grate of which was filled with pinecones. Mandy threw her weekend bag onto the bed. "We'll unpack later, okay?" she said to James. "Let's go and explore."

They wandered from room to room; some were heavily decorated, some were empty and echoing, and some smelled musty and old. James found a small library, in which few books remained; Mandy found a bathroom. The walls were covered with a faded green wallpaper, and the oval bath was carved out of a pale yellow stone.

"Gosh, isn't it amazing?" whispered James.

"Why are you whispering?" asked Mandy, groping for a light switch.

"I'm not sure," James confessed. "I feel like I'm intruding."

"We've been invited to look around, James!" Mandy said.

"Just a second. What's in here?" A door had swung open to reveal a narrow gallery of large, ornately framed paintings. Mandy was surprised to see an array of dogs

gazing out at her from the canvases. "Dogs!" she said wonderingly. "All dogs." They were all of the same breed — a big, proud-looking dog Mandy couldn't name. Her eyes scanned the room, taking in the fierceness and the expression of one dog, the gentleness of another, the unusual markings of a third.

"Wow, look at this one. It has a collar with a metal spike that . . . James? James!" Seeing she was alone, Mandy shot out of the gallery to find her friend tying his shoelace in the hallway outside. "Gosh, don't leave me by myself like that!" she scolded him.

"You're not scared, are you?" James grinned.

"Of course not!" Mandy said crossly as they walked

back toward their rooms. She didn't like to admit that she *had* felt a little strange in the room with all the eyes of the dogs looking out at her from the walls. "I wonder why there are so many paintings of dogs?"

"Somebody's collection, maybe? Mr. Blaithwaite's?" James added, "I don't think I've ever been anywhere so quiet!"

"Cheer up." Mandy smiled. "At least we'll be next door to each other. You can bang on the wall if you want. I'm going to go and unpack now. If we have an early night, then the morning will come more quickly."

James shivered, though he wasn't cold. "You're right," he said. "Good night." With a backward, questioning glance at Mandy, Blackie followed him along the hall.

Back in her bedroom, Mandy emptied her small weekend bag and was groping around for her toothbrush when Dr. Emily poked her head in. "Are you okay, sweetheart?" she asked, smiling.

"Isn't this castle wonderful, Mom?" Mandy said. "James and I found a portrait gallery full of paintings of dogs — all the same kind, too. Sort of like a greyhound, but with a thicker coat and a lot bigger."

"Sounds like a deerhound," Dr. Emily said. "They're related to the greyhound family. They were once used for hunting, I believe. Now, let's all get some sleep, okay? I've got a feeling tomorrow is going to be a busy day!"

Mandy woke up suddenly to the blackness of her room. For a second, she couldn't remember where she was, but the yellow moonlight that stained the sky reminded her. Skelton Castle! It was strange to think of being here, in the heart of a vast, ancient castle.

She lay still and listened. What had wakened her? Then she heard it. A thin, wavering howl, long and mournful, wafting on the warm night air. Her heart thudded painfully in her chest and she pulled the blanket closer to her. The noise stopped but, seconds later, she heard it again. Mandy got up and groped for the light switch, then she pulled on her bathrobe and stepped out into the hallway. She gasped when she saw James poke his head out around the door of his room. His hair was tousled and his eyes were big and round with confusion.

"What is it? Did you hear it?" he hissed.

"It sounded weird," Mandy whispered. "A catfight? A wolf, maybe?"

"There it is again," he said. "Sounds like a dog." Blackie was sitting up just inside James's door. His ears were pricked with interest. He listened intently, his head tilted to one side. Then he got up and began to pace briskly back and forth near the window seat.

"It's all right, boy," James told him.

"Should we go down the staircase and see?" Mandy asked. "It may be an animal in trouble."

"That's not a howl of pain. An animal yelps when it's in pain. It might be a dog far away howling at the moon," James suggested.

"There isn't a neighbor within miles of this place," Mandy retorted. "Unless you count that cottage we saw along the driveway. And if it isn't Blackie, then whose dog is it?"

"So which way do you suggest we go to find it?" James whispered.

"Oh, you're probably right," Mandy gave in. "Where would we begin in this huge place?"

"Exactly." They both looked at Blackie, who had stopped pacing and was lying down again. "Listen! It's stopped," said James, sounding relieved. "See? Blackie's settling down. I vote we go back to bed."

"Okay. But *wow*!" Mandy said, and let out a deep breath. "What a spooky start to our weekend at Skelton Castle!"

# *Two*

Mandy was glad when morning arrived. She hadn't slept well, and now, pulling on her jeans and T-shirt, she couldn't remember if she had really been awake listening for the sound of the howling or if she had dreamed it. The pale sunlight of Saturday morning came in from the window, warming the room and cheering it, making the strange noises of the night before seem unlikely.

There was a knock at her door. "Mandy, are you up?" James called.

"Not quite." She opened the door, then sat down on the bed to put on her sneakers. James yawned. Blackie's wagging tail beat a rhythm against the bed.

"I didn't hear any more suspicious noises last night after we went back to bed, did you?"

"No," Mandy said, smoothing the blanket and fluffing up her pillow. "It must have been the wind swooshing around the turrets of the castle or something."

"Maybe it's the plumbing," said James knowingly. "Probably old pipes. After all, the plumbing was probably installed —"

"James," Mandy said impatiently, "let's forget about it. We probably imagined the whole thing, anyway. Let's go and have breakfast. That way we'll be ready when Mr. Blaithwaite and Tilly arrive."

James ran his fingers through his hair. "Okay," he said. "You're right. And I'm starving. Come on, Blackie, you can go and explore the grounds now."

Making her way down the curving wooden staircase, Mandy marveled again at the age of the great stone walls that surrounded her. She was tempted to have another quick peek at the room where all the portraits of the great dogs were hung, but couldn't quite remember where the gallery was. James led the way along the hallway, beckoned by the warm yellow light from the kitchen at its end and the comforting smell of coffee and warm bread.

"Hello, you two." Dr. Adam smiled. "We were hoping

you would sleep late so we could eat your share of breakfast!"

"Dad!" Mandy said, grinning. "Wow, look at it all!"

"I told you I liked to cook." Ellie Booth chuckled, beaming fondly up and down the length of her table. The sight of the red-checked tablecloth, baskets of bread, rolls, and croissants and the assorted jars of jam was certainly welcoming. "There's eggs if you'd like, also sausages and bacon. Your mother tells me you don't eat meat, Mandy. That's all right with me, as long as you don't starve!" She gave out a burst of laughter. James then dragged up a wooden chair with a tremendous scrape.

"Sorry," he said, sitting down. "Did you sleep well, Dr. Emily? Dr. Adam?"

"Yes, thank you." Dr. Emily smiled. "Did you? On your first night in a real castle?"

"Umm," James began. "Did you hear anything last night?"

"Anything?" asked Dr. Adam. "Anything like what? Ghosts dancing a jig?"

"Oh, nothing," he mumbled. "Just the wind, I guess. You know, howling."

"It was a beautiful, still night last night," said Booth, coming into the kitchen with an armful of wood for the stove. "You must have been dreaming, James."

"We thought we heard a noise — like a dog howling," Mandy said. "It sounded so mournful."

Dr. Emily smiled. "Knowing you two, I'm surprised you didn't go off to investigate!"

"We *sort* of wanted to," Mandy said, "but we weren't sure where to begin in this big place." Dr. Emily laughed.

Mandy asked Mrs. Booth to name all the homemade jams. James cut a soft warm roll with a small sigh of pleasure. "Blackberry . . ." said Mrs. Booth, pouring coffee into Dr. Emily's cup. "That's marmalade — and that one is . . ." She broke off. The sound of car tires on gravel could be heard.

"They're here!" said Booth. Blackie pricked up his ears at the sound of car doors slamming and barked, his tail wagging expectantly.

"Oh! They're early!" said Mrs. Booth, quickly smoothing a few strands of graying hair into place. In the moment's silence that followed, Mandy became aware of a very loud noise coming from the direction of the kitchen window. A spine-chilling squealing could clearly be heard above a background of honking and shrieking. Added to this was the rumble of wheels on gravel and the revving and whining of engines.

"Good heavens! It sounds like a circus arriving!" exclaimed Ellie Booth, and she hurried out of the kitchen, her husband in tow. Dr. Emily and Dr. Adam, with

Mandy, James, and an exuberant Blackie, followed. Blackie ran ahead, clattering across the drawbridge, eager to investigate what sounded like a stampede.

Three medium-sized vans had pulled into parking spaces on the graveled open court on the other side of the drawbridge. Their respective drivers were now looking toward the backs of their vehicles at all the animals. Mandy and James — his hand on Blackie's collar — grinned at each other in delight, while Booth and Mrs. Booth hurried over with calls of welcome. Mandy was eager to see what was inside the three vans, but held back politely until some sort of order had been established. Then, at the crest of the curving driveway, proceeding at a leisurely pace, appeared an elegant silver-gray Rolls-Royce. Ellie Booth clapped her hands in relief. "He's here!" she said. "He's made it."

The stately car inched forward, and then the driver shut the engine and leaped out. He was a young man. He wore jeans and sunglasses and looked as if he could have been a rock star.

Mandy gaped. "Is that Mr. Blaithwaite?" she asked Mrs. Booth.

"No. Mr. Blaithwaite and Tilly are in the back." Mrs. Booth smiled. "That's Jack Stone, who helps Mr. Blaithwaite. Nice car, isn't it?"

Mandy didn't reply, because a boy of around her and

James's age hopped out of the back. He was tall and wore sneakers without socks. His jeans were cut off above the knee and his T-shirt was dirty and wrinkled.

"I thought," James muttered, "you said it was a grand*daughter*?"

"Who ever heard of a boy being called Tilly?" Mandy said in disgust.

"Hello," Tilly called from beside her grandfather's car and wiggled her fingers at them, her voice making it instantly clear that she was, in fact, a girl.

"It *is* a girl," Mandy said in a whisper. "At least, she's got a girl's voice. Let's go over." Tilly had fiery red hair that was cut extremely short.

"I'm so glad you're here," Tilly said pleasantly to everyone. "Oscar's been giving us a hard time!"

"Oscar?" said Dr. Adam, his eyebrows raised.

"My Vietnamese potbellied pig. He doesn't like car trips. He's glad we're here so he can get out." She darted down a hand to Blackie, whose tail thumped happily. "Beautiful dog, what's his name?"

"Blackie," said James, who, Mandy saw, was staring rudely at Tilly. Mandy nudged him discreetly. There was no need to stare, even though the girl's hair was shorter than James's and she looked as though she had slept in a tree.

"Well, I'm Tilly," the girl introduced herself. "I'm glad

you two could come for the weekend. Great place, isn't it?"

"Yes, it is. I'm Mandy, by the way, and this is my friend James."

"Come and meet my grandfather," said Tilly and she turned away, saying, "Gramps! Are you getting out?"

A tall, elderly man with lots of white hair eased himself gingerly out of his seat in the back. He was slightly stooped and leaned on a cane for support. He smiled, raising his stick, then staggered a little. Tilly put out an arm to him. "Grab onto me, Gramps."

Jack Stone was giving instructions to the drivers of the vans, but dashed over to Mr. Blaithwaite's side and helped to steady him.

"Thank you," he said to Jack. "You're very kind. How are they all? Have they arrived in one piece?" Jack Stone nodded and gave a thumbs-up. Satisfied, Mr. Blaithwaite looked up at Dr. Emily, Dr. Adam, Mandy, and James, waiting patiently to be introduced.

"Ah, you must be Dr. Emily and Dr. Adam! And Amanda, is it? And James? How good of you to come." He shook hands with Dr. Emily and Dr. Adam.

"Mandy," said Mandy, offering him her hand to shake. Blackie put a cold nose against Max Blaithwaite's hand, and he looked down in surprise. "Oh, hello, you handsome creature. Was I ignoring you?"

James stepped forward. "He's my dog, Blackie. I'm James. Thanks for letting him come along, Mr. Blaithwaite," he said.

"Ah, one more critter won't make any difference around here, my boy. There's plenty of room and no good carpets to soil. Have you had breakfast? Have Booth and Ellie been feeding you well?"

"*Very* well, thank you," Dr. Emily said.

"Splendid. Then I'll go inside and refresh myself briefly, if you don't mind, while Jack and the others unload the animals. Would you like to travel down to the yard with them? I'll join you there in time for an inspection. We didn't have any major catastrophes en route but I am anxious, nevertheless."

Tilly spoke up. "But you should have a rest first, Gramps. Your leg is hurting. You said so yourself."

"Nonsense, young lady, I'm fit as a fiddle." Mr. Blaithwaite ruffled Tilly's spiky, short hair affectionately. "Go on, and don't make a fuss over an old man."

"Okay, Mr. B.," said Jack Stone, who had removed his sunglasses. "I'll lead the other drivers around to the back and unload the animals now. I must say, they've all calmed down a bit since stopping. You shouldn't have any trouble. So, we'll see you around back in a while, okay?"

"Great," said Mr. Blaithwaite by way of reply. "See

you in a little while, Dr. Adam and Dr. Emily. So glad you could be here to help out. It's very reassuring."

"We'll go along and see them unload, okay? There won't be any room in the vans for us, so I'll take you through the garden." Tilly addressed Mandy and James. Mandy nodded. She couldn't wait to see Tilly's collection of pets — and she hadn't even had a chance to ask Tilly what kind of animals she had yet!

Minutes later, they had jumped over the great western wall of the castle, plunging down gleefully into the grassed-over moat bed and up the other side, to emerge in a garden grown wild from neglect. Tilly made her way along a small path, hopping over ditches brimming with thorn bushes and high, out-of-control weeds.

"You've been here before," puffed James, following Mandy. Blackie trotted behind him, his pink tongue hanging. He was loving this adventure.

"Gramps and I spent a day here a while ago with Jack. We had to set up a decent place for the pets to live. I discovered a shortcut to the fenced-in area. They used to keep horses here, years ago, and there were also kennels used for hounds. So it's perfect for us. Come on, if we hurry we'll be there before the vans." She began to sprint.

At the base of a gently sloping grassy hill lay a collection of crumbling old buildings, surrounded by elm trees filled with chirping birds. There were a few unused stables, painted a faded yellow, and several huts with grass growing on their roofs. The yard, Mandy saw, had been secured by smart split-pole fencing and a gate.

"Here we are," announced Tilly. "It's good, isn't it?"

"Perfect," Mandy agreed, as James inspected a small scratch on the back of his hand that he had gotten from a branch. The drivers, with Jack Stone, Dr. Adam, and Dr. Emily as passengers, soon appeared, entering the area by way of a dirt road to the south. They pulled in and parked as close to the various pet stalls as possible.

"Jack," Tilly called, "Oscar first, please."

"Okay."

A hush fell over the yard as Jack unhinged a ramp, then released Oscar. Mandy nearly burst with excitement as a very fat, black, potbellied pig came into the sunlight, blinking his tiny eyes in evident confusion and grunting loudly. His belly swayed as he neatly sidestepped down the footholds on the ramp. Tilly sprang forward, scratched his head fondly, then persuaded him to go into the stall with a handful of treats from her pocket.

Jack Stone and the other drivers were unloading each animal in turn. There were five Canada geese, several guinea pigs, hamsters, a small gray donkey, a llama, a peacock, a monkey, a large glass tank, or vivarium, brimming with Burmese tree frogs, and a huge South American iguana.

Mandy and James darted from animal to animal, as happy as could be.

"Look, James," Mandy said, thrilled, "he's licking my hand!" The llama was extremely tame.

"That's Suki, she's a girl," Tilly explained. "This is Duke, the donkey we bought from a man who sold his farm; that's Munch, the monkey. Oh, and the geese aren't so friendly, so careful." Jack led Duke into the paddock, and he brayed with pleasure at being let out of the van.

"Would you like to help us settle them in?" Tilly asked James and Mandy.

"Yes, please. We love this sort of thing," James said cheerfully.

"There's food in each of the vans, Mandy," Tilly said. "Could you haul it out and ask Jack where to put it, please?"

"Okay," Mandy said happily.

Just then, Mandy heard the purr of an engine and looked up to see Mr. Blaithwaite's Rolls-Royce being driven by Mr. Booth. He brought it to a gentle stop outside the yard.

"I hitched a ride," said Mr. Blaithwaite, smiling, coming across the yard slowly, leaning on his cane. "And how are they all settling in?"

"Very well, sir." Jack Stone grinned. "Oscar's calmed down. He broke free from his container in the van on the way up here," he explained to Dr. Emily and Dr. Adam, grinning. "The little troublemaker nearly had the van on its side!"

"He can be very hotheaded," said Mr. Blaithwaite.

"Max Blaithwaite, otherwise known as Dr. Doolittle!" Dr. Adam laughed under his breath. "What a collection of animals!"

When each animal had been released into the pen reserved for it, Dr. Emily picked up her veterinary bag. "All right? Are they all safely inside, Jack?" Jack nodded, securing the bolt on the last pen. "Come on, Adam," Dr. Emily said, "let's get started, okay?"

Dr. Adam began a brief clinical examination of each animal. "What signs do you look for?" Tilly asked, peering in over his shoulder as he grappled with Munch.

"For anything that might show us that they have suffered stress during their journey," Dr. Adam replied, leaning his forearm across Munch's wiggling neck to hold him still. Dr. Emily ran her fingers up and down the monkey's furry legs.

"No broken bones," Dr. Emily announced. "Mandy,

could you hand me my stethoscope, please?" Mandy delved into the bag. She knew exactly what she was looking for, having so often watched her parents work with animals in the clinic at home.

Dr. Emily listened to Munch's breathing and took his pulse. "Well, you've traveled happily enough," she told him. They moved on to Suki, the llama. Dr. Adam lifted her lips and looked at her gums. "What's that for?" Tilly asked, fascinated.

"If the gums are pale, it's a sign that the animal could be suffering from shock. But Suki here is in the best of health," Dr. Adam said. Duke did not like having his pulse taken, and butted Dr. Emily with his forehead. "Duke!" Tilly scolded. "They're only trying to help!"

Next the doctors checked the geese's wings. Dr. Emily's job was to cover the birds' eyes, to prevent panic and a possible attack, while Dr. Adam gently stretched open their wing feathers to examine the fragile, interlocking bones.

"James," Dr. Emily said, removing the cover bag from the first goose's eyes, as Adam finished checking it, "could you take a careful look around each of the stalls to make sure there is no ragweed that might be eaten by any of the animals? It's the tall, scraggly-looking plant with yellow flowers. Do you know which I mean?"

"Yup," James said, "I'll go and check."

"While we finish doing our rounds," Dr. Adam added, "will you and Tilly make sure there is clean water in all the troughs, Mandy?"

"Sure, Dad," Mandy said.

Max Blaithwaite, who had been wandering around greeting each of his animals in turn, came up to where Dr. Adam and Dr. Emily were now examining Oscar.

"When you've finished that, would you mind advising me on how to set up the vivarium, Dr. Adam?" Max Blaithwaite asked. "As you know, the temperature and the humidity levels have to be just right for the frogs to thrive."

"Certainly. I'm just about ready now," Dr. Adam said. "Oscar is a bit off-color after the trip. His gums are a little pale. Jack, let's make up a deep bed of straw to keep him cozy. Do you have any molasses or something like that to give him a bit of an energy boost?"

"Sugar cubes?" Jack asked.

"That'll do," Dr. Adam said.

"I'll go and get some." Jack strode away.

"Good job, Jack," said Mr. Blaithwaite. "Now, let me take you and Dr. Emily into this little hut, over this way. This is where we will want the vivarium set up." He limped off purposefully.

"They're almost all happily settled in. That's a relief," Tilly said, grinning at James and Mandy.

"How did you *get* all these animals, Tilly?" Mandy asked, watching her bucket fill with water.

"Gramps had some of them when I went to live with him three years ago, after my parents died. Then we just kept collecting more."

"Oh," Mandy said. She noticed that a shadow passed over Tilly's face and decided not to ask any more questions. But Tilly's face broke into a smile. "Come on." She made a fist and punched Mandy playfully on her upper arm. "Let me introduce Oscar to you — properly. He's a character." She looped her arm in Mandy's. Mandy looked over her shoulder at James and shrugged, smiling. He smiled back.

"Blackie!" James called. "Come on, boy. We're going in here."

Jack had broken open a bale of hay and spread it around for Oscar's nest. Tilly opened the gate to his pen. Mandy and James hesitated. "Come in," she urged. "He's harmless."

Oscar's little ears wiggled as Mandy and James entered his pen. His black snout moved furiously, absorbing the scent of his visitors. "Crouch down," Tilly advised, grinning. "See what he does."

"Hello, Oscar," Mandy said, kneeling in the straw. Oscar gave a grunt and trotted quickly toward her. Then he leaned his full weight up against her, pressing side-

ways, and Mandy, completely unprepared, toppled over. Tilly doubled over with laughter. Oscar pressed his slimy snout up against Mandy's cheek and grunted.

"He wants you to get up and scratch his back!" she chortled. Oscar sat down and set his tiny black eyes on Mandy. James put out a hand and rubbed his fingers up and down Oscar's thick, bristly neck. "His face is all squashed in." He laughed. "And he doesn't smell like a pig."

"Don't laugh at him." Tilly smiled. "He's a very sensitive pig. Aren't you, Ozzie? He loves baths. I scrub him with a brush, and he sways from side to side with pleasure." Oscar's charcoal-colored ears flapped comically as he trotted around the pen, then paused beside Mandy to sniff at her knees. "He likes you," said Tilly. "Here, offer him a treat." Mandy was still giggling as she held out a treat in the palm of her hand. "Where did you get him? He's adorable."

"He belonged to a neighbor of ours who had to move. He wanted to take Oscar to be sold! Gramps was horrified, so we bought him. He's very tame. He used to come in the house when he was little." Mandy, James, and Tilly took turns scratching Oscar in the places he liked best, while Oscar grunted and swayed around happily.

Blackie barked from outside the pen. "Sorry, Blackie."

James laughed. "I haven't forgotten about you!" Blackie tilted his head to one side, listening. Then, out of the corner of his eye, he spotted a small, wild rabbit nibbling at a mound of spilled grain in the yard. He couldn't resist. He shot out of the yard, yapping with glee, and ran after it in hot pursuit.

"Blackie!" James shouted. "Come back here! Blackie!"

# *Three*

"It was a rabbit, I think," James said. "I can tell by Blackie's excited bark. He's gone after it!"

"Oh, poor little thing," Tilly said. "Let's go after him. He might get lost on the estate if he chases it for long enough."

Mandy was just about to say that, knowing Blackie, this was unlikely. Then Tilly caught hold of her hand and hurried her out of Oscar's pen. Jack Stone was just coming in. "What's the rush?" he exclaimed, as the girls squeezed past him. "What's the rush?"

"Blackie's chasing a rabbit. We're going after him," Tilly yelled. James began to run after Tilly and Mandy, through the yard and across the hilly mounds of the estate.

The land was heavily overgrown in parts and smoothly barren in others. They skirted some old trees, ducking under low-hanging branches as they ran, trying to keep up with Blackie. The faster he ran, the more his pink tongue hung out, and the tone of his yapping grew more excited. It seemed to Mandy that she had been running for ages when, up ahead, Blackie suddenly stopped. She and Tilly and James were gasping for breath and holding their sides when they caught up with him.

Blackie was lying down at the foot of a decaying stone wall. It was buckled with age and its stones were home to a thousand varieties of small, creeping plants. It stood at about three yards high, too tall to see over.

"What's up, Blackie?" gasped James. "Did the rabbit get away?"

"He seems exhausted," announced Tilly. "Look at him — he's collapsed."

Blackie's dripping pink tongue danced as he panted heavily, but he looked extremely unsure of himself, as though he knew something the others didn't. He glanced around, head low, eyes darting. James stroked his head. "Hey!" he said. "There are plenty of other rabbits around to chase."

"What's behind this old wall?" said Mandy, who had leaned down to scratch Blackie's heaving chest.

"I don't know," Tilly answered. "I haven't been this far away from the castle before."

"Let's walk around it — there might be a gate," Mandy suggested.

They walked to where the wall made a sharp right-angled bend, then another, until they came to a high, double gateway. A closely woven pattern of wrought iron had served as a climbing frame for a mass of vines, but the gate hung ajar. Mandy squeezed through it sideways and Tilly followed.

"Blackie won't come," James called. "He's just lying there."

"He's tired," Tilly told him. "Leave him. He'll wait while we take a look, won't he?"

"Yes, I think so." James followed the girls through the gate. They stood in surprised silence at what they saw inside the crumbling old walls. Then Mandy spoke for all of them when she said, "Wow. What an amazing sight!"

Standing with their backs to the iron gate through which they'd come, they saw that the four high walls enclosed a small graveyard. Unlike the overgrown wilderness of the grounds outside, the green summer grass inside had been neatly clipped and carefully tended, so that each of the tiny headstones was clearly visible.

Tilly tiptoed forward, her hands clasped loosely behind her back. She bent down to read the inscriptions engraved into the rectangular gray stones above each grave. "Aminta," she murmured.

"Fifty little graves," James said frowning. "And one of them is recent," he went on. "Look, it's got fresh flowers on it."

Over in the corner, a fresh heap of earth hadn't had time to attract a covering of grass. The headstone bore the same unusual name: Aminta, and a bouquet of crisp white daisies lay across the mound, tied with a pale blue ribbon.

"Look at the dates," Mandy said. "This one over here is 1900 and I can only just make out this one. Wow — 1732."

"This latest grave is new," James said. "See? There's last year's date."

"Wait a minute!" said Mandy suddenly. "I remember where I saw the name 'Aminta' written now. You know that little picture gallery in the castle? With all the dog portraits? My mom said they were deerhounds. I didn't look very carefully or closely, but one painting I looked at — of a big gray dog — had 'Aminta' written underneath it."

"Hey! That's right!" Tilly breathed. "I remember going into the gallery when I first came here. All the dogs are called Aminta. It's written under every picture."

"I vote we leave now," James said, rubbing his hands vigorously up and down his bare arms. Mandy saw that he had goose bumps. "I want to see if Blackie's all right. He hasn't followed us in."

"Yes," Mandy agreed. "We could go back and ask your grandfather, Tilly. He might know about the graveyard and the name Aminta — or at least be able to help us to find out."

"Okay," said Tilly. "I'm thirsty after all that running, and we might have missed lunch. I'm glad that the rabbit got away, though. Come on!"

Blackie was lying in the same position outside the cemetery wall, waiting for them. He was no longer panting but seemed dispirited and disturbed. He got up when he saw James come out of the gate, but only wagged his tail once.

"What's up?" James asked him, puzzled by his unusually subdued behavior. "What is it?" Blackie's head and tail drooped.

"He must be tired," Mandy said, stroking Blackie's ears.

"Or thirsty," James concluded. "Come on, boy. We're heading back now." Blackie walked quietly and obediently beside James as they headed back toward Skelton Castle, each lost in their own thoughts.

They found Max Blaithwaite reclining in an easy chair in one of the living rooms, reading over a bunch of papers. He had his feet up on a padded stool and glasses on his nose. "You're back!" he said, looking up as Tilly burst into the room, followed by Mandy and James. "You've missed lunch. Where did you go?"

"James's dog went after a rabbit," said Tilly, "and —"

"Amanda, James, please help yourselves to a drink," Mr. Blaithwaite interrupted his granddaughter. Tilly went over to the table and helped herself to a glass of orange juice. "Anyone else?" she asked.

"Me, please," James said, stroking Blackie's head. His mouth was still dripping from the enormous drink of water he had had in the kitchen.

"Gramps," said Tilly, "we found the most amazing thing."

"What kind of thing?"

"A graveyard!" Mandy burst out. "We think it's a graveyard for *dogs.*"

Max Blaithwaite removed his glasses and crossed his feet at the ankle. "Dogs, huh?" he mused. "How did you come to that conclusion?"

"The gravestones are tiny," James explained. "Each

of them has the name 'Aminta' carved into it, and a date."

"All different dates," Mandy added.

"Gramps," Tilly said excitedly, "do you remember the gallery of paintings upstairs? All those pictures of dogs, all of them with little brass nameplates underneath? All of them — the dogs, I mean — named Aminta!" Tilly finished triumphantly.

"Yes," Mandy confirmed. "Isn't that a coincidence, Mr. Blaithwaite? And pretty creepy."

"And one of the gravestones had a recent date — last year — and the earliest one was 1732 — though it's faded," James added. Tilly was drinking her juice while walking round the room.

"Sit down, dear," Mr. Blaithwaite told her, covering his eyes with a weary hand. "Are you sure? I mean, I had no idea there was a graveyard on the estate! Why hasn't anybody told me about it? Where did you find it?"

Tilly explained the direction they had followed when they chased after Blackie. Max Blaithwaite then got up with difficulty and limped over to a pile of papers that lay on a polished mahogany desk. He began to shuffle through them, humming softly as he did so.

Mandy took the opportunity to look around the room. It, too, had floors of polished dark wood. They were so shiny that Mandy could see the arched windows reflected in them. Heavy oak beams supported the ceiling. A huge stone fireplace had seats on either side of the grate, and there were winged dragons carved into the stone mantel.

"Here we are," Max Blaithwaite was saying. "This is the map of the whole area that was given to me by the land registry office. Ah, now here — do you see this dotted black line running across here?" Mandy, James, and Tilly, who had crowded around the map, nodded. "That's the line of subdivision. It's a public right of way, and all the land on the other side of it — presumably where you have been today — is not land that belongs to me."

"That's the land that has been sold off?" Tilly asked, wrinkling her nose. "All that?"

"We saw that a trench had been dug and roped off when we arrived," James said, remembering.

"Yes," said Mr. Blaithwaite. "So, whatever it is you have come across is the concern of Mr. Peter Weeks, a London-based property developer who, I believe, intends to build six luxury homes on that land and turn it into a private estate."

Mandy was shocked. "But what about all those gravestones? Surely he can't just wrench them up out of the ground?"

"I'm afraid that's not your business, dear child." Max Blaithwaite looked gently at her.

"Well, somebody around here cares about those graves," James spoke up. "The grass has been clipped and the place well cared for."

"Perhaps someone from the town has wandered up from time to time," Mr. Blaithwaite trailed off.

"Fresh flowers have been laid on the most recent grave," Mandy said sadly.

Mr. Blaithwaite was studying his map again. "I can't understand why this graveyard you speak of doesn't appear on this map. If you say that it dates from around the time the castle was built, it certainly would be an important historical feature of the estate."

"We'll go back and take another look," Tilly began, jumping up.

"Now, you'll do no such thing!" Max Blaithwaite said sternly. "Tilly, dear, I beg you not to go exploring in places where you are not wanted. We have plenty of land of our own and enough to do to keep us occupied on it. Technically, you will be trespassing if you go onto Mr. Weeks's land. Now, let's put it behind us, okay?"

Tilly blinked at her grandfather. "Yes, Gramps," she said, sounding disappointed. Mandy was relieved when Jack Stone appeared in the doorway with her parents. The atmosphere lifted.

"Ah, hello there, Mr. B.," Jack began. "Bad news, I'm afraid."

"Ah, Jack! Adam and Emily!" Mr. Blaithwaite greeted them warmly. "What is it?"

"Oscar's run away, Mr. B." Jack shuffled from foot to foot, looking crestfallen. "The pen wasn't secure. He's been mean-tempered lately, as you know."

"What?" shouted Tilly, and then covered her mouth with her hands. "My poor Ozzie!"

"I'm sure he won't go far," Dr. Adam said quickly. "He's not a very healthy pig at the moment. Anyway, we've come back to organize a search party."

Tilly jumped up. "Quick! James, Mandy, let's go," she said. Blackie stood up and barked loudly, responding to the tone of urgency in Tilly's voice.

"Booth will help, too," Mr. Blaithwaite suggested. "I'll be down shortly to lend a hand. Oh, dear, things here seem to be off to a bad start."

"Sorry, Mr. B.," mumbled Jack.

"It's just one of those things, Jack. Arm yourselves with Oscar's favorite treats and let's do a thorough search, all right?"

"Right away, Mr. B.," Jack said, standing at attention. "Better leave Blackie up here, James, if you don't mind. We don't want *him* joining in the chase, do we?"

* * *

Tilly, who seemed to do everything in a hurry, had already sped down into the moat and vanished up the other side, calling: "Come on, you two!"

Down in the yard, she, James, and Mandy briefly inspected the damage Oscar had done to escape from his pen. "Look at that! He dug right under the wire — what a little escape artist!" James said admiringly.

"I thought he might be somewhere inside the yard helping himself to whatever snack he could find," Jack said, scratching his head, "but he's nowhere to be found around here."

"As I said, he won't have gotten far," Dr. Adam said reassuringly. "Pigs don't move very quickly."

"Yes," Dr. Emily agreed. "He's more likely to walk along looking for food."

"Still, there's no time to waste," Mandy urged. "Let's spread out and search."

Jack nodded. He seemed worried. "Thanks for your help, gang."

"If anything's happened to that pig I'll be really upset," Tilly mumbled, taking Mandy's arm.

"I'm sure we'll find him," James said cheerfully.

"Mom and I will head in this direction," Dr. Adam said, taking charge. "Jack, Mr. Booth, you head off that way. Mandy, you, James, and Tilly, try the woods. Okay?"

They went together into the thickets of trees —

birch, Scotch pine, elm, hazel, oak, and holly — stooping occasionally to gently part the bushes, in the hope that Oscar might have taken refuge there. "Oscar! Here, boy," Tilly called, and then whistled loudly. "Stand still and be quiet," Mandy suggested. "We might hear him running through the bushes." They stood statue-still, hoping. "Nothing," Tilly mumbled. She looked miserable. Mandy put an arm around her shoulders and they trudged on.

The sun had begun to slide below the horizon when James suggested they turn back and, wearily, Tilly and Mandy agreed. Mandy was worried about Oscar, but she tried to be optimistic and bright for Tilly's sake. They turned back toward the stable yard.

"Any luck?" Mandy asked Jack hopefully when they reached the yard.

"No, and it's almost dusk. We'll have to continue our search tomorrow. We've left a trail of food for him to follow. He might come back on his own."

Tilly sniffed, and Mandy could see she was fighting tears.

"I'm sure he will," she said hugging Tilly. "Try not to worry. We're all tired and it's been a long day of running around."

"I'm starving," James announced, rubbing his eyes. "We didn't have any lunch!"

"We're going to call off the search for now," Dr. Adam said, striding into the yard. "Look, Oscar should be all right overnight," he said, trying to reassure Tilly.

"He's having a small adventure of his own, Tilly. I wouldn't worry," Dr. Emily said kindly. "And I don't know about any of you," she added, resting her back against a split-pole fence, "but I'm ready for a nice hot bath!"

Jack Stone shrugged. He sighed, and Mandy could tell he was deeply concerned. "Yeah, I guess so," he said, taking off his cap and rubbing his eyes. "I'll go and report to Mr. B."

Tilly's face had been a picture of misery as they trooped forlornly back to the castle. She had shown no interest in Mandy's suggestion that they go and find the room in which the dog paintings were hanging.

"Try to look on the bright side," Mandy had said, "Dad says he'll find his way back home, and the estate *is* fenced in — he couldn't have gone very far."

Tilly had shrugged and given a half-smile, mustering her courage. Then, suddenly, she had brightened. "I know! Let's have a midnight feast tonight!" James and

Mandy looked at each other doubtfully, surprised by her lightning change of mood.

"No, honestly," Tilly insisted. "I'll plan it and organize it. It will be fun — and it will take my mind off Oscar."

Now, Mandy and James were sitting cross-legged on Tilly's bed, facing each other over a tray of treats neither of them could face eating. Ellie Booth had produced a hearty supper just two hours before — and James hadn't been able to resist a huge second helping. There had been plenty to eat, especially as Mr. Blaithwaite had not appeared for the meal, sending a message through Booth to say he would be retiring early.

"Try one of these cookies with chocolate on it," said

Tilly with her mouth full. She sat on an unpacked cardboard box, and behind her on the stone window ledge, the flame of a single candle flickered in the draft from the open window.

"None for me, thanks," said Mandy, patting her stomach. "I'm stuffed. But Blackie's interested."

Blackie's eyes were bright in the candlelight as he gazed longingly at the plate of sugary cookies and small iced cakes on the bed. He swallowed and licked his lips. Then, suddenly, his ears shot up in concentration and he tilted his head to listen intently to a sound they hadn't heard. James held out a cookie to him, but Blackie was completely uninterested. He went to the window, sniffed the night air, then began to pace, just as he had done the previous night.

"Oh, no," groaned James. "Here we go again."

"What?" asked Tilly.

"Listen!" Mandy said. "The howling!"

The high, mournful wail rose, it seemed, from the very depths of the castle and hung quivering in the night air. Tilly shot off her box, spilling her hot chocolate, and went to the window.

"A wolf!" she said triumphantly, leaning out. "It must be! How great!"

"Are you sure?" James whispered. "Here — I mean — on the castle grounds? Wild?"

"It can't be a wolf, just walking around like that," said Mandy. The animal howled again. This time the hair on Mandy's arms stood up and prickled. "James and I heard it last night before you and your grandfather arrived."

"Really?" said Tilly, and she dug into a bag and pulled out a wool sweater. "Let's go and investigate," she added decisively. "Come on, we have to find out what's making that noise. After all, if it *is* a wolf, it might eat Oscar!"

# Four

"Do you think we should?" James asked, glancing up at the window. It was pitch-black and the castle was eerily quiet, except for the persistent howl of the unknown animal.

"Come on, James," Tilly pleaded, blowing out the candle and snapping on the electric light. "This is a great adventure. We won't come to any harm."

Mandy stood up and pulled on her shoes. "Well, I'm more *worried* about that poor creature out there than frightened. It sounds to me as though it might need help. Come on, James. If we go together with Blackie, we'll be fine — we've got to find out what it is!"

"I was hoping," mumbled James, getting up reluctantly, "that we wouldn't hear it tonight." He looked across at Blackie, pacing back and forth below the window, looking unusually nervous. He began to pant slightly. Mandy hadn't seen Blackie do this before. He was always up for anything and more than eager for a challenge.

"It's not that I don't want to investigate, it's just that Blackie seems so . . . uncertain . . . as though he knows something, somehow, that we don't," James explained.

Ignoring James's protestations, Tilly grabbed a powerful flashlight from the depths of a grubby-looking knapsack. She put a finger to her lips and opened her bedroom door, which creaked alarmingly. Mandy and James followed her out. Their rubber-soled sneakers were soundless on the wooden floors as Tilly led the way to the top of the staircase. Blackie slunk along beside them, walking as though he expected the floor under him to cave in at any moment. He seemed very nervous.

"Why not take him back to the room?" Tilly said in a hushed voice. "He's going to wake the whole place with those tip-tapping claws of his."

James reluctantly did as Tilly suggested, shutting the door behind Blackie, saying, "You'll be better off in there, boy."

Mandy walked silently behind Tilly, glancing at the distorted shadows dancing on the walls in the light of her swinging flashlight. They found a light burning in the hall at the base of the stairs. Tilly plunged on excitedly, into the dark passage and beyond. Twice she paused, listening for the sound of howling, following it for clues to its source.

"It's coming from below us!" James whispered.

"There is a door to the side of the kitchen, and I know a flight of stairs leads to what my grandfather *thinks* is a cellar," Tilly said. "We'll try there."

Mandy couldn't tell if she was terrified or excited, but her heart pounded steadily as James and Tilly tried to budge the heavy wooden door. The moment it opened the sound of the animal howl could be heard loudly and clearly. "Howooooo . . ." It came floating up the stairs and echoing off the walls, as though someone had suddenly turned up the volume on a radio.

"Somebody," whispered James, "is playing a trick on us. This is a joke. There simply *can't* be an animal stuck down here!"

But James was whispering to Tilly's back. She was already leaping down the stairs in great excitement. Mandy noted how fearless her new friend was and, ignoring her own rising nervousness, followed quickly after her, with James on her heels.

At the bottom, the beam of Tilly's big flashlight showed a small, unused room without furnishings, except for a large, carved wooden chest. It smelled dusty and musty and made Mandy cough. Tilly swiveled the beam slowly around the bare stone walls. The howling had stopped.

"Are we dreaming, or what?" Tilly said softly.

There, in a corner, an enormous dog was sitting calmly and expectantly on the floor. It had the same smallish head and elegant body of a greyhound, only a bit larger, and with a thick, ragged pale blue-gray coat. It sat still, gazing at Mandy, James, and Tilly with a sort of quiet dignity. It seemed to be sizing them up.

"A deerhound!" Mandy breathed.

"How on earth did it get down here?" Tilly said, amazed.

"Who can it belong to?" James whispered.

"It looks just like the dogs in the paintings!" Mandy said. "It's one of the Aminta dogs!"

"Well, it isn't going to attack us, that's for sure. It looks as gentle as a lamb. I wonder how long it's been trapped down here?"

"It couldn't have been long. It doesn't look thin or anything," James observed. "Perhaps it belongs to someone who keeps it in here and comes to feed it."

"That's cruel!" Mandy said. She moved past Tilly and

cautiously took a step toward the dog. But nothing about the great dog's expression or behavior seemed threatening. It didn't get up, or growl, or bare its teeth.

"Hello, you sweet thing," Mandy spoke gently and held out her hand. The dog stood up and took a step backward. Mandy saw that it had a snow-white mark in the shape of a diamond on its chest. "We're not going to hurt you," she told it softly. "Come on and say hello. Good dog."

"Definitely mysterious," James said. "I mean, it's not frightened or angry, it isn't wounded or sick — so what's it doing sitting down in this chilly old room making all that noise?"

The dog took a few steps toward the wooden chest. It moved gracefully, almost as though it were gliding. Again, Mandy reached out, shuffling slowly forward on her haunches, a low hand outstretched. "Here, boy." But again the dog moved back a pace out of Mandy's reach, still looking steadily at her.

"I can't see a water bowl or any food around, can you?" Tilly asked, flicking her flashlight around the corners of the room. The dog now began to sniff, then paw at the wall against which the big chest was standing. It looked up at Mandy and tilted its head, then pawed at the wall again, making a scraping on the stone with its claws that made Mandy's hair stand on end.

Tilly crouched low and aimed the beam of her flashlight on the dog. "It's a girl dog," she announced. "Anyone can see that."

"She doesn't want us to touch her, but I think she's asking us to open this chest!" Mandy guessed.

James came forward. "Shine your light on the bolt, Tilly." He bent down and examined it. "Hmm, it's padlocked — no hope of opening it." The dog had backed off into the shadows when James had approached. Now she came slowly forward, put out her elegant front paw and scraped at the wall again.

"No, she wants us to move it!" cried Tilly. "Let's push it over — she's lost a ball or something, I bet, behind it."

James pushed hard against the chest with his forearms. It gave easily, sliding along on the smooth stone floor. "Look!" breathed Tilly. "There in the wall!" A small, bolted opening about one square yard had been revealed.

James tugged at the bolt, working it back and forth until it opened with such force that it knocked him back onto the floor. Laughing, Mandy and Tilly helped him up. "Wow," he said. He turned around to look up at Tilly. "Maybe we should get your grandfather, or someone."

"No, not yet," Tilly said. "I vote we go in and take a look."

"Shine your light over there first, Tilly," said James. "Let's see where the dog is. Oh, look, she's gone. She's gone through the door."

"She couldn't have, James," Tilly said. "The door isn't even completely open yet." The unbolted door had swung open only a few inches. She shone the light around the room, directing its beam into all the corners. The dog had gone.

"This is *weird*," said James, with a shudder.

Tilly was on her hands and knees, the metal casing of her flashlight hitting the stone. She had pulled open the doorway and was starting to crawl through it. Her voice came back to them from the other side of the wall, sounding as though she was speaking with tissue paper in her mouth. "She's here waiting for us. Come through. Oh! It's a dungeon!"

Mandy and James had been plunged into sudden and complete darkness.

"I'm on my way," James said quickly and dropped to his knees. Mandy followed, groping her way behind James.

The stone was so cold it felt slimy. Mandy could hardly believe she was slithering through a passageway in the basement of a creepy castle in the middle of the night, scrabbling after a mysterious dog that didn't seem to be real. She wondered briefly if she might be dreaming, then, as she struck her shoulder hard on the frame of the doorway, realized she was wide awake.

James was sitting just inside the small opening, hugging his knees. It was extremely cold. The room was small and square, and made entirely of stone.

"Gosh," James breathed, and a cloud of condensation rose around him from his own warm breath. "It's a real dungeon, where they used to keep *real* prisoners!" Mandy stared around. Metal rings were bolted into the stone wall. James raised his arms and slipped both wrists into the shackles, and hung there with his chin on his collarbone.

"Ugh! James, don't!" Mandy begged.

"Please, James," Tilly said. "Where's the dog?" She moved her flashlight beam away from James.

The dog had retreated to a shadowy corner of the room and, to Mandy, seemed to be waiting patiently for their next move.

"Just look," Tilly cried. "Look at all these old books and things here on this shelf." James began to cough from the dust that was disturbed by Tilly's searching hands. "There are maps and recipes — all in funny handwriting — and marvelous, heavy old leather-bound books. How amazing!"

"Tilly," Mandy said softly, "let's follow her, okay? There'll be a chance to look at those some other time."

Mandy pointed to the dog, who was now standing with her back to them, staring into the gaping mouth of an arched doorway, the metal-barred gate of which hung open. As Mandy spoke, the dog slowly turned her small head in their direction, then looked back into the passageway and stepped purposefully into darkness.

James scrambled to his feet. "Let's not lose her!" he said.

"She wants us to follow her, I'm sure of it," Mandy said. "She seems to be taking us somewhere!"

Reluctantly, Tilly moved away from the shelf of treasure and pointed the beam in the direction the dog had taken. Mandy suddenly couldn't bear the thought of not knowing where the beautiful creature had come from, or where she was going. She and James ran into the passage beyond the doorway, Tilly close behind them. They hurried after the dog, who moved quickly ahead of them, looking back over her shoulder from time to time to make sure they were following.

On and on they went. The rough and uneven stone floor of the tunnel made the going difficult, and twice Mandy almost fell. James, in the lead, now held the flashlight, which threw out an arc of light showing a damp, moss-covered ceiling. Water trickled down the walls. They walked downhill for a while, then the tunnel floor evened out before it rose steeply uphill.

"We must be going under the castle moat," Tilly said, her voice echoing eerily.

"We must be crazy, doing this," James said. "We might be getting ourselves into danger and . . ."

"Oh, don't, James," begged Mandy. "Don't spoil it. It seems this dog has a mission of some kind. She wants to share it with us. We can't let her down. And after all, we have come this far."

"I suppose so," stuttered James, through chattering teeth.

Up ahead of them, a warm glow of yellowy moonlight was creeping into the tunnel mouth.

"Look!" said Mandy. "It's moonlight — it must be where the tunnel ends." They hurried toward the light. Mandy was eager to see if the dog would be waiting for them.

"Oh," she said. "Look where we are — again! We're back in the cemetery! And we went all this way and through all this trouble!"

Outside, the sky was velvet dark. The brilliance of a huge yellow moon meant James could switch off the flashlight and save the batteries for their long journey back. They stood gazing around them, at the neat rows of tiny gravestones, lost for words.

"Why did she bring us here?" Mandy whispered. "Where has she gone?"

Then the dog appeared at the iron gates to the cemetery, her long curved tail moving slowly from side to side. Once more she turned around and headed off into the darkness.

"Oh, no," groaned James. "She doesn't expect us to follow her, does she?"

"Yes, she does," Mandy said firmly. "And I'm going to follow, that's for sure. Are you coming?"

# *Five*

Gusts of wind blew through the high, dark trees. Mandy was pleased to be out of the tunnel and into the fresh, moonlit night air. She inhaled deeply, wondering briefly how moles could bear to be underground for such long stretches of time.

"You know," said James, "that we are now trespassing on the area of land your grandfather said had been sold off."

"We won't tell him," Tilly said quickly. "It would only worry him, so we won't say anything. Let's just keep this secret for now, okay?"

"Yes," Mandy agreed. "I think we should. Come *on*,

you two, the dog's still waiting for us to follow. Look at her!" Tilly and James looked over to where the dog waited patiently in front of the gate, her back to them. Occasionally, she glanced at them over her shoulder. In the dark, with the tree shadows dancing across her coat, she looked almost unreal.

"All right," said Tilly, "let's go." She marched forward and immediately the dog slithered gracefully through the iron gates. James yawned a great, gaping yawn.

"How can you be tired, James, at a time like this?" Mandy wondered.

"Well, maybe because it's about one o'clock in the morning," James retorted. Then he went on: "You know, Mandy, maybe this dog is just a stray. She wandered into the castle by mistake and now wants to go home."

"If she were a stray," Mandy reasoned, "I don't think she would have been so aloof. She would have been much more needy and nervous. No, it's almost as if she had been *expecting* us. Calling for us."

"Weird," James said again. He turned on the flashlight. They had entered a shallow grove of oak and beech trees that shielded them from the moonlight. Mandy could only just make out the shape of the dog ahead, moving like a streak of smoke through the trees. *She isn't like a normal dog*, Mandy thought. *She doesn't bark or whine or fuss or leap or even wag her tail as most dogs do. She's patient and dignified and, well, different.*

Reaching the outskirts of the grove, Mandy turned to see Skelton Castle on the hill, huge and pink-looking in the moonlight, pale against a frame of black night.

"Can you see her?" Mandy whispered to Tilly.

"No, and heaven knows where she's brought us. I mean, where in the world are we now?"

"Listen!" James had clutched Mandy's arm to stop himself from stumbling over a stone. "It sounds like water."

"We're near the lake!" Tilly said, dumbfounded. "She's brought us to the lake. I saw it marked on Gramps's map."

Mandy squinted her eyes in the half-light for a sign of the dog, but there was no trace of her presence now. Suddenly, a squealing sound sliced through the silence of the night and made Mandy jump. Tilly clutched Mandy, who clutched James, and they stood dead still to listen. There was the sound of gentle lapping, and a squelching, like somebody in rubber boots walking through mud.

"Oscar!" shouted Tilly. "It's Oscar! Come on." She raced across a grassy field over the rise of hills and down to the lake, which was still and inky-black. Mandy and James scrambled after her. The squealing, now accompanied by frantic sucking sounds, got louder.

"Give me the flashlight, quick," Tilly commanded. The beam of yellow light highlighted the reflections of the trees wavering in the breeze beyond the shore and Oscar, up to his shoulders in thick, oozing mud. His stubby snout moved frantically as he snorted and squealed in terror, his tiny piggy eyes wild with the effort of his struggling. "Oh, Ozzie!" said Tilly, her voice filled with tearful relief. "You silly, silly old pig! Just look at you." At the sound of her voice, Oscar stopped struggling and slumped back into the unpleasant-smelling silt.

"I'm so glad we've found him," Mandy said, wrinkling up her nose.

"He's really stuck," James observed. "Poor Oscar. Who knows how long he's been in that smelly stuff!"

"We've got to get him out," Tilly said, then added: "It's all right, boy, we're right here on the shore. We'll help you." Tilly flashed the beam around, looking for inspiration. The light landed on a boat jetty, standing tipsily in the mud on tilting wooden stilts.

"He must have walked along the jetty from the shore and fallen through," Mandy said. She could see several large gaps where wooden planks should have been.

"I'll bet this jetty hasn't been used in years," James said, peering from behind Tilly's shoulder. "It looks rotted through."

"Take off your belt, James," Mandy said.

"What?"

"Take off the belt on your jeans!" Mandy repeated. "We'll loop it around Oscar's neck and pull him out."

"He'll be strangled," James said.

"But we've got to do something!" Tilly said despairingly. Oscar squealed loudly and thrashed around in the mud. It held him like glue.

"Well, let's give it a try." James unbuckled his good leather belt. "Oh, gosh," he said. "This is awful."

"It'll wash out," Tilly said. "Don't worry."

"I'm not worried about the belt," James told her. "I'm concerned for Oscar." Dutifully, James knelt to remove his sneakers, which, even in the moonlight, Mandy could see were coated with slimy ooze. She looked around again for the dog, looking into the bushes and even across the water of the lake, but there was no sign of her. She was gone. "The dog seems to have vanished," Mandy said. "She did us a favor, though, didn't she, bringing us to Oscar?"

"Yes, we would never have found him in time if it hadn't been for her," Tilly said.

"Oscar probably would have suffocated in this icky

stuff by the morning," James said, holding his nose. "Struggling to get out would weaken him and eventually he'd have collapsed."

"Oh, don't, James, please," Tilly said. "Let's go! Are you coming, Mandy?" Mandy slipped off her shoes. She was grateful that it wasn't a chilly night. Nevertheless, the first contact of mud on her bare feet was a shock, and Mandy gasped at its cool, clinging touch.

"Oh, yuck!" said James in disgust. "This is gross!"

They waded in, the mud closing around their ankles and calves. *It's like walking through chocolate pudding*, Mandy thought, *but much more smelly*. But she was so relieved that they had found Oscar that she

didn't mind. The pig's little eyes swiveled frantically in his head as they got closer, but he kept still, breathing hard from his efforts to escape. James slipped his belt round Oscar's thick neck, then looped the end through the buckle and tightened his grip. Oscar grunted loudly in surprise.

"All right," said Tilly. "Good job, James. Let's all pull together." Six hands began to pull and tug. Oscar gave a mighty snort as he was dragged onto his side and the smelly mud got all over his cheek and ear.

"Oh, no!" cried Tilly. "All we're doing is getting him in deeper!"

James plunged his hands into the mud and lifted Oscar's head out. It came out with a plop that sent mud flying across James's face.

Mandy took off his glasses and cleaned away a splash covering one lens with her sleeve. She replaced them. "Thanks," James said gratefully. "Look, this isn't working. We'll have to get help."

"Yeah, I guess you're right," Tilly said, looking sadly down at her pig. Oscar, exhausted, was slumped miserably, panting hoarsely. "Wake up Jack, not Gramps, all right?"

"And Mom and Dad, too," Mandy said.

"Me?" James asked.

"Please, James," Tilly pleaded. "I want to stay here

with Oscar and I'd like Mandy with me. Do you mind?" James shook his head.

"You know where the kitchen is?" Tilly asked him. "Jack's is the room right next to it. You'll find it. We'll stay here and watch Ozzie. Go as quickly as you can, okay?" Tilly's voice was desperate.

James picked his way slowly out of the mud. As he moved away, the flashlight faded and Mandy felt a chill creep down her spine. *Please*, she pleaded silently, *let the moon stay with us until he returns!*

It seemed to Mandy that hours had passed before she heard the distant, welcome voices of Jack Stone, James, and her mom and dad. She and Tilly had huddled together on the shore, a yard away from the mud where Oscar was stuck like a beached whale. They had their arms around each other for comfort and warmth. Their feet were crusted over with drying black silt. She and Tilly had been too wound up to sleep. They had kept a watchful eye on Oscar, in case he sank like a stone. The moon had stayed with them, casting a rippling glow across the far-off water of the lake, lapping just out of Oscar's reach. "If this was a lagoon," Mandy had said, "then the tide would have come in by now and we could've floated Oscar out of trouble!"

"No such luck," Tilly had said, hugging Mandy closer.

"Hey, I think someone's finally coming!" Mandy had exclaimed a few moments later.

The two girls got shakily to their feet. "James!" Mandy shouted. "Over here." Dr. Adam was first to come crashing across the grassland and onto the shore. He was closely followed by Jack Stone. James jogged along behind with Dr. Emily.

"Are you all right, sweetheart?" Dr. Emily hugged Mandy and handed her and Tilly a second sweater each.

"Thanks. I'm fine. But poor Oscar, Mom, he's exhausted and so frightened!"

"Thank goodness you found him. Silly little pig!" Jack said. He steadied the flashlight and focused it on Oscar, who looked like a big black lump. Mandy, shivering like jelly, thought he looked like an old barrel.

"Oh, Jack," Tilly said. "I was so scared that he'd drown. He must have fallen through the wooden slats of that boat jetty."

"We'll get him out," Dr. Adam said. He had a spade in his hand.

"Thanks so much, James," Mandy said, giving her friend a thump on the back. "You've been great."

"Yes," Tilly said. "Thanks."

James was breathing hard from his run back to the castle. His arms were covered with a bunch of tiny scratches. Mud from the lake had dried on his legs and down one side of his face. "Poor James," Mandy mumbled sympathetically.

Jack and Dr. Adam had plunged into the mud. Jack held his spade above his head. James followed them in, and immediately made a face from the smell. Jack began shoveling the mud away from Oscar, filling the space with gobs of it and dumping it aside, while Dr. Adam held the rope collar he had slipped around the pig's neck. Oscar squealed in terror, nervous about what was happening to him. The tops of his legs became visible, then the hoof of one stumpy foot. Dr. Adam worked around his hind legs, and within minutes, Oscar was free.

"Hooray! Hooray!" chanted Tilly, as Oscar was lugged to the shore by Jack, whose legs were buckling under his enormous weight. "I can't hold him! He's too heavy!" he said, putting the pig down.

Dr. Emily, waiting at the edge of the mud, stepped forward and slipped the rope from around Oscar's neck. She passed it under his muddy stomach, tying it efficiently into a harness. "Lead him along on that," she told Jack. "It won't strangle him this way." She stooped to examine Oscar, who was limp with exhaustion. Dr. Emily ran her fingers up and down Oscar's legs, scraping the cloying mud away with her fingernails. After a minute, she stood up.

"I'm afraid he did more than just get stuck in the mud," Dr. Emily said gravely. "He's got a huge gash down the side of this back leg. It'll need stitching."

"Oh, poor Ozzie," Mandy said. She looked at James. From his pale, tired face, she guessed he'd had enough excitement for one night.

Tilly scratched Oscar's head. "Don't worry, Ozzie. We're going to take you home and make you better."

"Let's head over to the yard now," Dr. Adam suggested. "I'm going to need your help with getting Oscar there, Jack. We don't want him to put any pressure on that leg, if we can help it."

"You go on ahead and get yourselves cleaned up, then wake up Mrs. Booth and ask her to make a pot of coffee for us, will you? I hate to wake her, but we need to attend to Oscar immediately and I feel I need something to keep me going," Dr. Emily said, looking at Mandy, James, and Tilly.

"Yes," said Tilly brightly, as though it were about nine o'clock in the morning and she had just gotten out of bed. She rolled down the legs of her filthy jeans and started walking to the castle.

Mandy and James followed Tilly, who still had a spring in her step. Mandy felt as though she was sleepwalking, but she was very relieved Oscar was safe. Her mom and dad would have him back to normal in no time.

"Hey! Just a minute, you guys," Jack called after them. "I forgot to ask you. Just how *did* you find Oscar out in the lake in the middle of the night?"

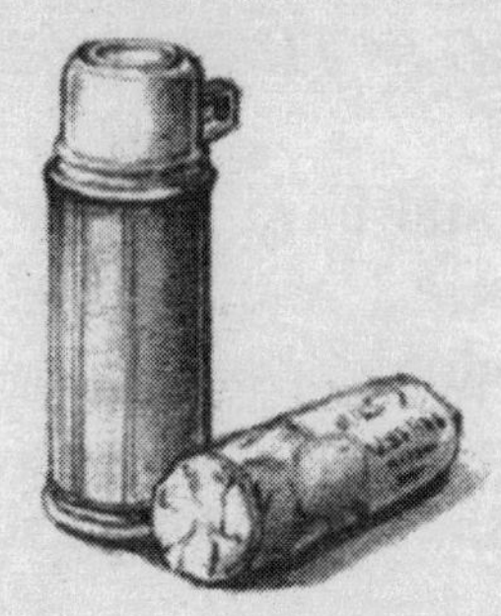

# *Six*

Lights went on all over the castle as Booth and Mrs. Booth were awakened with the news of Oscar's rescue. Ellie Booth decided not to wake Max Blaithwaite, thinking she'd surprise him with the good news of Oscar's rescue in the morning. "He needs his rest," she reasoned, filling the coffeemaker with water, "and there isn't anything he can do at this hour, except worry."

Mr. Blaithwaite slept on as Tilly, Mandy, and James took turns in the bathroom and put on clean clothing. "He uses earplugs," Tilly confided to Mandy, who was scrubbing at her legs with a sponge. "The whole castle could crumble to the ground and Gramps wouldn't know a thing until he was hit by a falling brick."

"I'm really glad you've cleaned up," Booth observed, looking at James's, Tilly's, and Mandy's legs. "I thought I'd been wakened by the Loch Ness monster when I first saw you standing at the door of our room, James. And what an awful stench!"

"So did Blackie," chuckled James. Blackie's tail thumped against James's legs. He seemed to think that they were about to go for a walk. A walk was always welcome, even if it was in the middle of the night.

"It's a very good thing you found Oscar," said Mrs. Booth, as she bustled around pouring sugar into a small airtight container. "I'm so delighted the silly old pig is safe."

"We'll take the car and drive around to the yard," Mr. Booth said decisively. "I expect you've had enough walking for one night. Are you coming, Ellie?"

"I'm ready," she replied, stuffing a packet of cookies under her arm.

"Sorry, Blackie," James said, ruffling his dog's fur, "but I'm exhausted."

They found Dr. Adam and Dr. Emily with Jack, clustered around Oscar, who was lying in a small pen, in deep straw, on his good side. Dr. Adam had cleaned most of the mud off him and made him as comfortable as possible, but the gaping wound on his leg was open and bleeding. "Oh, my poor Ozzie," Tilly said, covering her eyes. The Booths greeted Jack, who was sitting beside Oscar, stroking his ear.

"We really need another light," Dr. Adam said. Booth stepped forward and directed a powerful beam of light onto Oscar's wound.

"Thanks," said Dr. Adam, opening his black vet's bag.

"Ugh," said James. "That looks really nasty."

"Oscar, boy, don't worry," Mandy called softly. "We're here to make you feel better." She pushed gently at Blackie, whose nose was twitching to absorb the smell of this strange, grunting creature lying on the ground.

"Yes, it's as Dr. Emily thought out at the lake. We'll need to stitch that up," said Dr. Adam, probing gently at the wound.

"But won't it hurt him?" Tilly said, in a small voice.

"I'll give him a local anesthetic so he doesn't feel a thing and also a sedative so he doesn't decide to go exploring again halfway through my handiwork!" Dr. Adam said. He took a bottle out of his bag, filled a syringe with a pink-colored liquid, and injected it into Oscar's thick neck. Oscar lifted his head and grunted, then flopped it back onto the straw.

"That will take about ten minutes to work," Dr. Emily said, stooping to lift one of Oscar's little eyelids to peer into his eye. "So we have time to get organized." She handed Dr. Adam a plastic bag of fluid.

"Oh, are you going to put him on an IV?" James asked.

"No. This is an IV drip bag — you're right about that, James, but I'm just going to use this sterile fluid to wash the mud out of his wound."

Oscar was now lying peacefully, breathing deeply and evenly. Dr. Adam filled a second syringe and injected it into the skin around the deep cut. Then he cleaned his hands carefully with a pack of sterile wipes and eased on a pair of tight plastic gloves. Meanwhile, Dr. Emily used the bag of sterile fluid to flush away the mud, using the syringe to squirt the liquid just where it was needed.

"Let's have some light over here, please, Booth." The beam was directed onto a rolled-up cloth of shiny silver instruments, and from it Dr. Adam selected a scalpel.

"Ooh," said Tilly. "I can't watch." Mandy put an arm around her shoulders.

"I'm only going to clean up this jagged-edged wound, Tilly," said Dr. Adam. "Then we'll stitch it up and he'll be as good as new."

"I'll prepare an antibiotic injection," said Dr. Emily. Mandy saw that Tilly was looking away from where her father worked on Oscar. She was gazing out at the night sky.

"Look," Mandy said, "it's starting to get light." There was a rim of faint orange light on the horizon. James yawned.

"I'm exhausted," he said.

"Coffee, Dr. Emily?" said Mrs. Booth, offering a mug.

"Oh, that's great, thank you," she replied.

Mandy accepted a mug and went to stand beside her mother. She badly wanted to tell her mother about the beautiful dog they had found who had led them to Oscar and saved his life by doing so, but she didn't want to let Tilly down. Tilly wanted the dog to be their secret. She decided to say nothing.

"You still haven't told me how you found Oscar," Jack said suddenly.

"Tomorrow," Tilly said quickly. "It's far too late for any more talking."

"Early," said James. "It's too early, you mean." And he yawned again.

"You three go to bed now," Jack suggested. "You've done a good night's work. You've saved Oscar's life, that's for sure. I'll let Mr. B. know the happy news as soon as he wakes up."

"Thanks, Jack. And thank you, Dr. Adam and Dr.

Emily," said Tilly. She linked arms with Mandy and James. "Come on, team." She grinned.

James whistled and Blackie's ears pricked up. He took a final quivering sniff at Oscar, then scampered after them.

When Mandy woke up, the sky she could see through her bedroom window was the same pale and hazy orange it had been when she had fallen asleep. She looked at her watch, puzzled. It read 6:00 P.M. Sunday evening! She had lost a whole precious day at the castle while in a deep, dreamless sleep. She dressed quickly and sped down the stairs two at a time.

In the kitchen, Tilly, James, Max Blaithwaite, and her parents sat around the large oak table. Booth was preheating the oven while his wife chopped up vegetables for dinner. Blackie sat looking up at her with large shining brown eyes.

"Wow," said Mandy, "I've been asleep for hours. Sorry."

"We've all had our share." Dr. Emily laughed.

"Mandy, my dear," said Mr. Blaithwaite, who had half-risen to his feet when Mandy came in. "Your parents and Tilly have been filling me in on the details of Oscar's rescue. All of you were very brave. You did a great job."

"How is he?" Mandy asked, sitting down.

"Fine," said Dr. Adam. "Jack has proved himself a good nurse and reports that Oscar is up and about already, looking for a way out."

"No chance of that," Tilly put in. "Jack's covered every possible escape route."

"Tilly has been telling us, too, about your adventures after dark," Dr. Adam began, "and she . . ."

"I said how we couldn't *wait* to explore the grounds, which of course, we did." Tilly widened her eyes at Mandy and put a discreet finger to her lips. James was studying his fingernail. Mandy didn't know what to say, so she smiled and nodded. *It wasn't exactly a lie*, she thought. *We certainly did have an adventure!*

"Well," Dr. Emily said, taking a basket of rolls from Ellie Booth, "now that you have had your little adventure, there will be no need to leave the castle at night, will there?"

Mandy, James, and Tilly looked at each other. "Probably not," agreed Tilly. "When's dinner, Mrs. Booth? I'm starving."

They sat up late playing cards in Mandy's room. Blackie, who had spent a busy day down in the yard with Jack Stone while James had been sleeping, now snored gently at the foot of the bed. Mandy was wide awake and even James looked alert and fully recovered. "I hope that she comes back," said Mandy. "I mean, it would be such a shame if we never saw her again."

"Who?" asked James absently, shuffling his hand of cards.

"The Aminta dog. She was amazing," Tilly agreed. "I just wish I knew where on earth she came from and how she managed to find her way into the dungeon."

"The way she led us to Oscar was creepy," James said, with a small shudder.

"Do you have to leave tomorrow?" Tilly asked suddenly. "Wouldn't Dr. Adam and Dr. Emily let you stay on a little longer, so we can solve the mystery together?"

"We could ask," Mandy said, her eyes shining. "It would be great to stay. I'd hate to miss out on seeing Aminta again."

"Me, too," said James. "Let's ask — after all, it is our school vacation."

"Let's go back — now!" Tilly said, jumping off the bed and spilling the pile of cards.

"Back where?" James said, looking alarmed. "That smelly lake?"

"No! The room where the old books are! Let's go and see what's in them!"

"Yes!" said Mandy excitedly. She couldn't help hoping that the dog would be waiting for them. Blackie lifted his head, alerted by the tone of Mandy's voice. He yawned and struggled into a sitting position, blinking expectantly, then scratched his ear lazily.

Tilly was putting on a sweater, so James quickly scooped up the cards and put them into a pile. He looked doubtful. "Stay here, boy," he told Blackie. "Go back to sleep. Creeping around down there will only make you nervous again."

Tilly took the flashlight and led the way down to the kitchen and along to the staircase leading to the basement. A light shone from under the door of Jack Stone's room and Mandy heard the muffled sound of a radio playing softly. As they tiptoed past, Mandy thought briefly about her mother and father. She wasn't disobeying them, she told herself. She was not, after all, going to be leaving the castle.

At the foot of the stairs, Mandy's heart began ticking like a bomb that was about to go off. Her eyes scanned the corners of the basement room in the dim light, hoping for a glimpse of the dog.

"No sign of Aminta," said Tilly.

"Well, she probably wandered back to her home by now and is curled up by her owner's fire dreaming of being lost in Skelton Castle," James whispered. Mandy was a little disappointed. They crouched and shuffled through the tiny doorway, which was still ajar, and Mandy grabbed the first of the old books that she came to. A cloud of dust rose around the heavy old leather binding. Tilly and James crowded around Mandy as she began to turn the yellowed, crisp, parchment pages.

"The writing's difficult to make out," Mandy said.

"Let me see." James took the book from Mandy and sat down. "Point the light on the page, Tilly." James looked closely at the elaborate, curly writing in big black strokes on the pages and began to read: "'I am the happy owner of three of the noble breed. A fine litter born this day of January 12th, 1770. Two males (Glen and Monarch) destined for the kennels of the Marquis of Hithestowe (as deer trackers) and one female, a rough, lightish-gray color, which I intend to keep here at Skelton Castle, to be named Aminta, from the Greek, meaning protector.'"

"Wow," breathed Mandy. "Aminta — that name again. This is somebody's diary."

"Probably the first Lord Skelton to have owned and lived in the castle, judging from the date — the eighteenth century. Gramps told me that's when the first Skeltons came here."

"Do you think your grandfather knows about these books?" James whispered.

"I'm sure he doesn't." Tilly said. "And they might be valuable."

"Listen!" James said, after he turned two pages of the book: "'I have survived . . .'" James squinted in the dim light and struggled to make out the strange script, "'this day the boating accident that took the lives of two men and three of my best hounds, among them Cohmstrie, as good a tracker as ever ran, and Buscar, who was thoroughbred, the best that ever I saw of any kind, save my beloved Aminta, whose courage this day shall not go unrewarded.'"

"Read on!" Tilly urged excitedly. "How did Aminta show courage?"

James mumbled to himself as he skipped over a few lines he couldn't make out. Then, at the bottom of the page, he read: "'She showed signs of exhaustion after her brave rescue and had swallowed much of the waters of the lake. Fistfuls of her coat remained in my clenched palms long after she had dragged me to the safety of the shore, where we lay gasping till Donaldson came upon us at the break of dawn.'"

"Wow," Mandy said again, her eyes as round as saucers. "What an incredible tale. She saved him from drowning."

"It doesn't add up," Tilly said, frowning. "I mean, why

are there so *many* graves in the cemetery, all with the name Aminta on them?"

"Yes," Mandy frowned. "And all those portraits of the same type of dog in the little gallery."

"Let's try another book," James suggested. "We're bound to find out more. There are all sorts of books here. This is a log of some kind," he read. "There's a map in here and some old records."

There was a fizzling sound and a small pop, and the beam of the light went out, leaving them in complete darkness.

"Oh, no," Mandy said, in a very small voice. "The battery's dead."

"Yikes," said Tilly. "Now it really *does* feel spooky in here."

"Hold on to me, Tilly, and you, too, James," said Mandy, groping around to feel for her friends. They made contact, clung for a moment, then began to inch their way in the general direction of the little doorway leading back to the basement. James struck his head on the wooden chest coming through and cried out loudly.

"Shh!" Tilly cautioned. "We don't want to wake Jack."

"Tilly," Mandy said, as she gratefully reached the bottom of the stone staircase leading up to the castle, "we're going to have to tell your grandfather about our discovery in the dungeon. About the books and the dog."

"She deserves to have a name," James said. "If we ever see her again, we'll call her Aminta, okay?"

Tilly and Mandy nodded. "Aminta," they said together, and then climbed the stairs to their rooms in silence.

# *Seven*

Max Blaithwaite was stacking books from a packing crate onto shelves in the library when Mandy, James, and Tilly found him the following morning. Booth, who had carried up his breakfast on a round silver tray, had the job of reaching deep into the box and hauling out the heavy volumes one at a time.

"Aha! A joy to see you all on this beautiful morning. Have you had breakfast?" Mr. Blaithwaite beamed a sunny smile and, without waiting for a reply, went on: "Your parents are due to leave today, Mandy, and I believe are taking you two away with them, is that so?"

"Gramps," Tilly said. "Can they stay? Here, I mean? For a day or two? Something's come up, you see."

"Come up?" He looked puzzled.

"We've made an amazing discovery, Mr. Blaithwaite. We want to talk to you about it, if you have time," Mandy said, putting a restraining hand on Blackie, whose curious nose was sniffing in the box.

"All the time in the world, Mandy. And of course you can stay as long as you like at Skelton Castle — with your parents' permission. Booth, another pot of coffee, if you please."

Booth straightened, with a faint groan, and rubbed his back. "Certainly, sir. Shall I let the dog out onto the grounds?"

"Thanks," James said. Blackie was being treated royally and was having the time of his life. He wagged his tail when Booth called and trotted after him happily.

"Come and sit down," Mr. Blaithwaite suggested, "and you can tell me all about it." He eased himself into a scarlet velvet armchair facing the huge, gaping mouth of an empty fireplace and smiled with anticipation. Mandy thought how wonderfully cozy the square stone room would be in the winter, with a roaring fire going. She sat on a small Oriental rug beside the hearth. James squeezed up beside her, while Tilly paced around on the polished floorboards.

"Gramps," she began. "We've been exploring the castle this weekend." She paused, as though wondering where to begin. Max Blaithwaite had propped his chin in the palm of his hand. *He looks so wise — and interested*, Mandy thought.

"There's a dungeon down below the kitchen, and there are some amazing books in it," Tilly said.

"Records," James put in.

"The musical variety?" Mr. Blaithwaite asked, clearly puzzled.

"No, Gramps, *books*! Old books about Skelton Castle, all sorts of things."

"There's a diary, written by a Skelton family member, we think, which tells the story of a drowning and about how he was saved by a —"

"A wonderful, big brave dog — a deerhound, like the ones in the picture gallery," Mandy finished James's sentence. Mr. Blaithwaite held up a hand and smiled, his eyes closed.

"Stop!" he ordered. "My poor head is spinning. You must take me to this Aladdin's cave of treasure at once, so I may see for myself just what it is you have discovered. It could be of significant historical value."

Just then, Booth, bearing a silver coffeepot and several cups and saucers on a tray, opened the heavy oak door to the library. Behind him were Dr. Adam and Dr. Emily.

Mandy thought how sad it would be if she never got a chance to see Aminta again and hoped her parents would allow them to stay for a few more days.

"Mmm, is that coffee I smell?" Dr. Emily asked.

"Come in, help yourselves. Have you had breakfast?" said Max Blaithwaite.

"We've had the usual Mrs. Booth feast, thank you!" Dr. Emily laughed.

"I'm so grateful to you both," Max Blaithwaite said. "It's been marvelous having you around to oversee the settling-in process. And, of course, to help with Oscar."

"Ask them, will you, Gramps?" Tilly urged her grandfather in a low voice.

"Uh? Oh, yes. Tilly wondered if it would be all right for Mandy and James to stay on a little longer. It's great company for Tilly and there's plenty of room, as you know!" Dr. Adam and Dr. Emily looked at each other for a few seconds.

"No more getting bogged down in muddy lakes at midnight?" Dr. Emily asked, looking at Mandy.

"I promise," said Mandy, grinning.

"We'll be back here ourselves in a day or two," Dr. Adam said, dropping a lump of sugar into his cup. "To check on Oscar's leg. So we can pick you two up then. If you're sure, Max?"

"Absolutely," Mr. Blaithwaite confirmed. "How splendid, that's settled then. And will you two be staying for lunch?"

"No, thank you." Dr. Emily smiled. "We'll start our trip home after coffee. It's been a marvelous weekend."

Mandy and Tilly could hardly contain their impatience while the farewells were being said. Booth took forever loading the weekend bags into the Land Rover. Then Blackie jumped into the car and stubbornly refused to get out again, convinced that James was going to drive away without him.

"Go inside," prompted Ellie Booth, chuckling. "That way he'll know you'll be staying with us." James went into the kitchen and Blackie, looking very alarmed, leaped out of the car and followed him at a trot. Then, at last, when the Land Rover pulled away down the long driveway, Max Blaithwaite stopped waving and immediately turned to Tilly. "All right, now. Lead on! Take me to your dungeon."

"Oh, Gramps, we're so excited!" cried Tilly. "I'll go and get my flashlight."

"It needs new batteries!" James yelled, as she sprinted away.

"I know!" Tilly yelled back.

* * *

It took Max Blaithwaite a while to walk down the stone steps leading into the basement. Mandy was certain that when he saw the tiny doorway to the dungeon he would refuse to go through it. Instead, he muttered: "Oh no, are you sure?" And at James's vigorous nodding, he managed to squeeze through.

"Light," shouted Mr. Blaithwaite when he reached the other side and found himself in pitch-darkness.

"Coming through," Mandy called, slipping through the tunnel-like opening with ease.

"I've got your cane, Gramps," Tilly said, following. James appeared soon after, with Blackie at his side. Tilly shone her rejuvenated flashlight on the shelves against the wall. They stood in triumphant silence. Max Blaithwaite let out a long, low whistle of pure amazement.

"My goodness! What a find! Why, we may never have discovered this dungeon if you hadn't moved that chest aside. I expect it has a gory past. If only walls could speak."

"I'm glad they can't," Mandy whispered, imagining she could see blood dripping onto the stone floor from the handcuffs attached to the wall. Max Blaithwaite limped over to the pile of leather-bound, cobweb-strewn books, stacked precariously on the ancient shelves.

"Well, well, well, what an astounding find," said Mr. Blaithwaite again, exhaling a huge puff of air in astonishment. "Tilly, my dear, just *how* did you discover this place?" He coughed and blinked, looking around in amazement.

"There was this eerie howling on Saturday night. We thought it might be a wolf. We followed the noise to this room and found . . ."

"A deerhound in the room next door," Mandy finished. "She was beautiful. She wouldn't let us touch her but she wanted to get in here — she made that clear enough."

"A stray? Locked in? Here?" Max Blaithwaite asked, horrified.

"We're not exactly sure," James said. "She led us out, though — through that archway there, and down a long underground tunnel, into the cemetery and on down to the lake where Oscar was trapped."

"But this is all absolutely extraordinary," said Mr. Blaithwaite, clearly dumbfounded by the secrets harbored by his castle. "The dog must have found her way in through the tunnel, surely? She was after the smell of food wafting down from the kitchen, no doubt."

There was the sound of knee joints cracking as Max Blaithwaite bent down to pick up the first volume. Mandy, James, and Tilly fell silent while he began carefully turning the crisp parchment pages. Mandy saw that his bushy eyebrows had been drawn together in a frown of amazed concentration.

*Aminta,* Mandy pleaded to herself, looking into the darkened corners of the cold and musty-smelling room, *please come back.*

"Aminta," said Mr. Blaithwaite, keeping his eyes on the book, "is the dog that saved Hector Skelton's life. This is a diary of some kind, written by the man himself. It says here that she was buried in the castle graveyard in 1732. She was twelve years old."

"That's the date we saw carved on one of the tombstones!" James said, excitedly.

"Not the one with the fresh flowers on it?" Tilly asked, openmouthed.

"No, that one had a more recent date on it," Mandy said. "Remember?"

"Keep the flashlight still, Tilly dear," her grandfather urged. "Let me read. It says, um, let me see . . ." Max Blaithwaite began to read. "'Nothing could exceed the courage displayed by my Aminta on that day, having struggled through the waters in a most determined way; and whose selfless actions have saved my life. I hereby decree that all future owners of this great castle of Skelton must keep on the land one or more of the breed, seeking out those who are long in body and light of foot — a breed held in such high esteem — to protect the castle . . . a talisman of luck throughout the days to come — and to be lain in the ground at their life's passing in the burial site where my beloved Aminta now lies, a sacred and fitting resting place for all of the castle's valiant protectors . . .'"

Blackie whined, making Mandy jump. James stroked his head and he lay down with a heavy sigh. "Blackie's cold," James announced. "He's shivering all over."

Max Blaithwaite was unraveling a tightly folded parchment map, hand-drawn in black ink. "Here, look," he said. "There's the cemetery which you told me about — and, of course, the cemetery of which this man Hector writes. It's clearly marked. And yet it's missing from the map given to me by the land registry office."

"Isn't it wonderfully spooky?" Tilly said, thrilled.

"It's more than spooky," said her grandfather, carefully storing the ancient map away in the protective folds of the book. "It means that I've got some work to do. I certainly won't be responsible for allowing this important piece of history to be sold off for modern housing. I shall have it stopped immediately. I'll go to court if necessary . . ."

"Hooray!" shouted Tilly, leaping up and down.

"I think Blackie wants to get out," said James in a small voice. "I don't think he can breathe in here, or something." Mandy saw that Blackie was panting and beginning to pace back and forth. She suddenly felt hopeful — this was exactly the way Blackie had behaved when he had heard Aminta's presence through her howling. She looked around again but could see no sign of the dog she now automatically thought of as Aminta.

"Should we take the books upstairs so we can take time to look over them?" Tilly asked.

"No," Mr. Blaithwaite replied. "We can't risk damaging them. They've been hidden away down here in the dark for so many years, let's leave them. I intend to come back and examine them at my leisure."

"I'll take Blackie out now," James said.

"Yes, I feel the need for some air myself. Let us return through that unpleasant little opening in the wall. I want to call my lawyer right away," said Mr. Blaithwaite, feeling for his cane.

James, with Blackie, went through first, and Tilly held the flashlight for her grandfather. Mandy had stooped to a crouching posture when she glanced back over her shoulder a final time at the arched entrance to the tunnel. She gasped. The great dog was sitting

quietly in the tunnel mouth, statue-still, looking back at her through eyes gleaming gold in the fading light. Mandy was overjoyed. Her heart began to hammer with excitement.

"Aminta," Mandy said softly. "Good girl, Aminta." At this, the dog tilted her head deliberately to one side, listening intently. "Tilly! Look!" Mandy said urgently, clutching and pulling at Tilly's T-shirt. Tilly looked back, just in time to see the dog stand and slowly walk back into the tunnel and disappear.

"Oh, she came back! Gramps, James!" Tilly shouted. "The dog was here!"

"Shh!" said Mandy. "You might frighten her."

"Well, she's gone again now," Tilly said, and slipped through the doorway after the others. Mandy followed reluctantly. She couldn't stay alone in the dark, though she badly wanted to follow Aminta down the tunnel.

Upstairs, Max Blaithwaite, breathing heavily from climbing up from the basement, limped off to his study to contact his lawyer on the telephone. "I'll report back!" he called.

Mandy sat down on the landing. She said to the others: "Aminta came back! She can't be a stray, she just *can't* be. She's here for a reason. Let's go to the gallery and look at the dog portraits, okay?" Tilly and James nodded eagerly.

"I think I remember the way," James said, looking at Blackie's wagging tail in relief. He ran after them as they hurried up the staircase to the second floor. "This way," said James. "Along here and in . . . here!"

"Good job, James," Mandy said, as James turned on the light switch, bringing the windowless little gallery to life. They stood clustered at the heavy wooden door, gaping, as a hundred painted eyes gazed back glassily at them from the walls. Mandy looked along the row of portraits until she came to the one of the deerhound with the distinctive white diamond in the middle of her chest.

"There!" cried Mandy. "There she is — there's our

Aminta." They all looked to where Mandy was pointing. Though they had only seen her at night, by flashlight, Mandy was suddenly convinced that this was the portrait of the dog in the dungeon.

"Look at that white diamond on its chest," James breathed.

"It's exactly the same," Tilly said. "That's the picture of the dog in our dungeon, no doubt about it."

# *Eight*

"I wish you'd stop meddling in the past!" Ellie Booth pleaded. "There's no point, Tilly — no good will come of you snooping around down there in the dark, digging up buried secrets."

Sitting at the kitchen table, Tilly sighed as Ellie plunged another dinner dish into the steaming water of the basin. "Your poor, dear grandfather," Ellie Booth muttered on, scrubbing vigorously. "Goodness only knows what this will do to his health."

Mandy scooped up her empty plate and James's and took them over to Mrs. Booth at the sink. "Thanks for a great dinner," she said with a smile, watching Blackie licking up the last traces of rice from a bowl that had been put down for him.

"Gramps is fine," Tilly asserted, scoring patterns gently on the tablecloth with her knife. "He's just trying to do the right thing. As soon as he can get hold of his lawyer, then we can save the burial ground of the castle's dogs."

"Graveyards! Ghost dogs! Howling in the dungeon! I don't like it, I don't like it one bit!" Mrs. Booth said firmly, her cheeks flushed pink from fervor and the heat in the kitchen. Tilly ignored her. Her eyes shone with excitement. She sipped a glass of juice and said: "Do you *really* think the dog could be a ghost?"

"Well, it doesn't seem to eat, or drink," James pondered. "I mean, there's no food dish or water bowl around, is there?"

"She," Mandy corrected. "She, James, not *it.*"

"She, then," James said.

"The dog in the painting is her exact replica. I suppose that's possible," Mandy reasoned. "Dogs can look alike. There may be another living stray dog around that looks just like her."

"But remember the way she managed to slip through the doorway into the dungeon, the first time we went down — and it was only open a few inches!" Tilly said.

"Hmm . . . the way she appears suddenly, then vanishes," Mandy added. "And won't let us touch her."

"Enough!" said Ellie Booth, thoroughly perplexed. "We'll all be having nightmares in our beds. I'm off to mine right now, and you should be, too."

"In a while," Tilly said. "We'll turn the lights off down here when we go, okay?" Impulsively, Tilly jumped up from the table and gave Mrs. Booth a hug. "Don't *worry*!" Ellie Booth shook her head, frowning.

"I don't like it," she said again, and left the kitchen to go to bed. Tilly sat down. "Should we play cards?"

"I don't really feel like it," Mandy began, then sat straight up in her chair, her eyes wide.

"Howoooooooo . . ."

They waited for the dying echo of the howl to finish. Then, Mandy slapped her palms down on the table in triumph, startling James. He put out a hand for Blackie, wanting to comfort him. "There you are," Mandy said. "She's come back for us. Should we get the flashlight?"

"I'll go!" said Tilly, jumping up.

The howling came again, much louder than they had previously heard it, because now they were directly above the basement that led to the dungeon. Goose bumps prickled along Mandy's arms. Blackie began to pace, panting hard.

"Here we go again," James said, tying his shoelace. "Who knows where we may end up tonight." He chuckled. "Scotland, perhaps?"

"You *want* to go, don't you?" Mandy asked him.

"Yeah, only, I wish she'd come in the daytime. Why does it always have to be dark?"

"Yes," Mandy agreed, "that's another strange thing about her."

Aminta howled again as Tilly appeared in the kitchen with the flashlight. "Spare batteries," she puffed, showing the pack to James. "Let's go!"

"I'm going to leave Blackie here, in the kitchen," James said. "I don't want him to be scared."

"Good idea," Mandy said, stooping to plant a kiss on Blackie's soft head. "Don't worry, boy. Go back to sleep — we'll be back soon."

Mandy ran to the fridge and snatched up a slice of roast beef left over from dinner. *Hang on, Aminta*, she said to herself. *We're coming.*

The arc of the flashlight shone on Aminta in the shadowy, farthest corner of the basement, wedged between the right angles of stone wall.

"Hello, girl," Mandy said softly.

The great dog looked more blue in color than Mandy remembered. She carried her head high, and her yellow gaze was level and calm. She didn't stand up and wag her tail in greeting although, Mandy thought, she knew them all now and might have been expected to do so. Her neck was long and arched and her thin, shaggy tail lay still and curled on the floor in the shape of the letter C. Instinctively, Tilly, Mandy, and James held back, though Mandy longed to approach her.

"Wait for her to guide us," Mandy whispered to the others. They waited, huddled in the semidarkness, and Mandy became aware that Tilly was holding tightly to the leg of her jeans in excitement. Mandy loosened Tilly's grip, crouched, and tossed the slice of roast beef across the floor. It landed with a little plop at Aminta's feet.

"What's that?" hissed James.

"Meat," Mandy answered. "Let's see if she's hungry." But Aminta showed no interest at all in the tasty morsel beneath her nose. She moved neither to investigate its scent nor to eat it. Instead, she stood and stepped delicately, gracefully, along the far wall, so that Tilly had to follow her with the flashlight. She glided through the small doorway to the dungeon beyond. They looked at each other, then scrambled after her.

"The chase has begun," James said melodramatically, brushing dust off the knees of his jeans. "I hope that Oscar is safely in his bed tonight!" he chuckled.

"Yeah!" Tilly laughed, very softly. Mandy thought it was strange that none of them wanted to risk offending Aminta by making any noise.

"She trusts us," Mandy said. "She really trusts us and I'm sure she's trying to tell us something. Are we agreed that we'll follow — wherever she wants us to? I think it's too important *not* to."

James hesitated for only a second before he nodded. "Agreed," he said solemnly, glad that he had left Blackie in the kitchen.

"Agreed," Tilly repeated. "Hold this, will you?" She passed the flashlight to James, who went on ahead.

Aminta stood by the arched doorway, looking back over her shoulder as though silently urging them to follow her down the passage to the graveyard. They hurried over the sloping stone floor of the tunnel, breathing in the damp smell of centuries past. Mandy felt her way with her feet. She hesitated to put out a hand to the ancient, curved walls, fearful of small creatures buried in the crevices of the rock. "Ugh," said James. "Look at these cobwebs."

The circle of light was like a halo above Aminta's sleek head as she trotted along purposefully, her claws tapping on the stone floor. When the stale air in the tunnel began to smell fresher, Mandy knew they were near the end and felt relieved. The moon had turned the cloudless sky a midnight blue in color and cast a ghostly light over the tombstones in the cemetery. "Thank heavens for the moon," said Mandy.

"Look," said Tilly. "The white daisies are gone from that grave. Someone's put some different flowers there instead."

"Honeysuckle," Mandy observed.

Aminta again paused at the cemetery gate, then slipped ahead, moving like quicksilver, on down through the tangled copse of trees. They hurried after her. Mandy's jeans were snagged by a bush; Tilly was pricked by a thorn. "Ouch!" she said, but didn't slow down. "Keep up, James, will you? We don't want her to get away."

"She'll wait for us," James said, trying to direct the flashlight's beam so that they could all see where they were going.

"Look!" Tilly said. "She's sitting down. Is she resting?"

They formed a group, carefully maintaining a good distance between themselves and Aminta. She sat statue-still, looking ahead of her. Then Mandy saw what it was Aminta had brought them to. The vast, hulking body of a backhoe towered above the tallest tree. Its garish yellow body looked horribly out of place among the soft greens and earth colors in the woods. The metal neck of the machine arched and stretched toward the ground, the huge bucket poised to strike, like some ghastly prehistoric monster.

"Oh, no!" James said. "The machines are going to demolish the graveyard!"

"I hadn't realized the work would begin so soon," Tilly gasped. "This is awful."

"Look," said Mandy miserably, "there are white slashes of chalk on these old trees. That probably means they're going to be cut down, too."

"There's another, and another," Tilly cried. "Oh, they're going to get rid of all of them." Tilly walked from one doomed tree to another, rubbing with her fingertips at the chalk in an attempt to wipe it away. All she succeeded in doing was smearing it.

Mandy stood staring around her as Tilly and James moved away with the flashlight. She stood in a pool of pale moonlight, feeling the weight of sorrow inside her like a stone. Aminta sat with her back to Mandy, waiting patiently. "Aminta!" Mandy called softly. "Aminta, I'm so sorry for you. They're going to take your graveyard away, girl. But we're going to help you, I promise. We'll do everything we can — and Mr. Blaithwaite is going to stop it. He said he would."

Just then, James and Tilly came running back. "They've hacked away all the ivy from the cemetery gate," James said, flashing the light in Mandy's face. "They really mean business."

"Hey," said Mandy, "you're blinding me with that light."

"Sorry," James said. "Oh, look, Aminta's leaving again." Mandy got to her feet and Tilly linked arms with her.

"Don't look so upset," she said to Mandy. "We're going to stop this before it goes any further."

Aminta was moving ahead, walking carefully through the leaves of curly copper beech and around the sturdy bulk of thick oak trunks. They hurried to catch up to her.

"We're going a little too far," James cautioned, after a further fifteen minutes. "I don't think your grandfather would be too happy about this."

"Aminta won't lead us into any danger," Mandy said, convinced that she was right. "We'll be all right, James," she added, although she, too, was beginning to wonder just where they were headed. Aminta appeared to be quite certain of the route she was taking across the vast grounds of Skelton Castle.

"It's getting late," James said, pausing to look at his watch. "It's after ten o'clock — I think we ought to turn back."

"No," Tilly said. "Look, down there — she's stopping."

Aminta had trotted down the sloping side of a grassy

bank and stopped at the bottom. Beyond her, Mandy could see the moonlit outline of a drystone wall in need of some repair. A thatched roof with one leaning brick chimney stuck up above it reminded Mandy of a feather on a hat.

"It's that small cottage we saw when we first arrived. We must be near the main gates," she said in surprise.

"There are a few houses marked on Gramps's map," Tilly confirmed. "I've seen them. But I didn't know that anybody was *living* in them!" Lights were burning in two of the downstairs windows and through the first, larger window, they could see a woman at a table, sewing. Aminta was sitting directly outside the wooden front door, looking up at a large brass knocker expectantly.

"Do you think this is where Aminta lives?" James said incredulously.

"Surely she can't have brought us all this way to meet her owners!" Tilly said.

"No," Mandy asserted. "I don't believe that for a minute. I think she wants us to go in."

"Go in?" James exploded. "We can't! We don't know them, they don't know us. We might frighten them if we knock at night — and what will we say?"

Mandy didn't answer because at that moment, Aminta lifted her paw and scraped long and hard at the

door. Immediately, the woman in the window put down her sewing and stood up, a puzzled frown on her elderly face.

"Now we're in for it," hissed James. "Let's go!"

"No!" Mandy cried. "Wait. Look."

Aminta had vanished — melted away in the darkness as though they had, after all, imagined her. There was the sound of the key turning in the lock, and the door ground open with a protesting creak from an unoiled hinge. Light from the room spilled out into the night.

# *Nine*

An old man stood at the door of the cottage, looking out into the night, an expression of surprise on his face. He glanced up at the moon, then from side to side. "Is anyone there?" he called in a thin, wavering voice.

Mandy hesitated for a second, then she stepped out boldly from behind a bush on the crest of the hill. James tried to grab her, but she was too quick for him.

"Hello," Mandy said loudly, wondering if the man would be able to hear her. "Over here." She waved. "I'm sorry to bother you, but . . ." She ran down the hill and stepped through a section of the wall that had crumbled. "Do you own a dog — about this high?" She held the side of her hand against her rib cage. "With a shaggy, blue-gray coat?"

"A deerhound?" said the man in a rasping voice. "There aren't any more of them around here. Not now." He looked at his wristwatch.

"I'm really sorry." Tilly smiled, stepping forward. "We shouldn't have bothered you. I'm Matilda Blaithwaite, from Skelton Castle, up on the hill there." James had made his way slowly to the front porch of the cottage. Mandy felt as though she had a wild bird trapped in her chest, her heart pounded so fiercely. Yet, to her surprise, the man didn't seem at all angry at their late-night intrusion.

"I know who you are," he said. "You're the granddaughter of the new owner. We wondered when you'd visit, but we didn't expect it to be in the middle of the night!"

"We're sorry," Mandy repeated.

"Who is it, Tom?" The woman they had seen sewing in the window appeared at his side. She wore a robe. "My goodness! It's children. Out at this time of night! Come in, come in!"

"They were looking for a lost dog, Molly. A deerhound," the man said, standing aside as Tilly, Mandy, and James shuffled into the tiny hall.

"I'm Molly Noble and this is my husband, Tom," said

the woman. "I'll put up some water. Do you want something warm to drink? How about some hot chocolate? You've walked quite a distance if you've come from the castle."

Mandy and James looked at Tilly, who shrugged at them and made a face. "Why not?" she whispered. "We might find out some more about Aminta."

"It is sort of late for us to be visiting, Mr. Noble," Mandy said. "We can come back another time, if you'd like."

"My wife and I are poor sleepers. We generally stay up late, so don't worry about keeping us up. Does your grandfather know you're out and about so late?" He glared at Tilly.

"Sort of," Tilly mumbled. Mandy had a sudden vision of Max Blaithwaite asleep in his room at the castle, unaware that his granddaughter and her friends were out roaming around the grounds. Yet Mandy felt certain, somehow, that Mr. Blaithwaite would approve.

"Here we are, then," said Mrs. Noble, shuffling in with a heavy tray. She set it down on a table in the living room. "Sit down, please."

Mandy sank gratefully onto a worn rug and rested her back against a sofa. She hadn't realized until this moment how tired her legs were. James sat cross-legged on the floor and Tilly sank into a big armchair with a heavy sigh. "Wow, it's good to sit down."

"We're so glad you came, aren't we, Tom?" Molly Noble smiled warmly at her husband. He nodded.

"Now what's this about a lost deerhound?" he asked.

"We don't know who she belongs to, Mr. Noble," Mandy spoke up. "She's a gorgeous dog who kind of comes and goes . . ."

"We followed her here, to your cottage. This is where she seemed to want to be. It was the dog who scraped on the door for your attention, not us," James put in.

"Ah, yes," said Mr. Noble dreamily, looking at the beamed ceiling. "Do you know about deerhounds as a breed?" Mandy, James, and Tilly shook their heads. Mrs. Noble handed them each a mug of hot chocolate.

"They look fierce, but are as gentle as doves on the inside. They're as fast and powerful and fearless a breed as you'll get. The Phoenicians were said to have brought the first deerhounds to these shores as hunting dogs way back in the year 1000 B.C., and as they moved north, they developed a thick coat, for warmth." Tom Noble paused to sip his tea. *He was clearly enjoying having someone to talk to*, Mandy thought. "Deerhounds were used in Scotland to hunt deer and stags in the Highlands. They were favored by Highland chieftains. Anyone below the rank of earl was forbidden to own one."

"Tell them about Aminta, dear," Molly Noble said, delicately stirring a lump of sugar into her tea. Mandy sat up straight; Tilly's mouth dropped open. James swallowed a mouthful of hot chocolate too quickly and nearly choked.

"Ah, Aminta," Tom Noble said and paused, looking sad. "There's always been a deerhound or two at Skelton Castle, until now, that is. Molly and me, you see, we worked for the last Miss Skelton, who lived in the castle before your grandfather bought it."

"Miss Amelia Skelton," Mrs. Noble said. "She was as kind as could be. I was her housekeeper for years, and Tom was the groundsman."

"Oh," Tilly said. "We didn't know that. But we knew Miss Skelton had died."

"The first Sir Hector Skelton, who owned the castle many years ago," Tom Noble said, "was saved from drowning by his faithful deerhound, Aminta. That's the way the story goes, anyway. You can take it or leave it." Mandy, James, and Tilly exchanged glances. They already knew this part of the story to be true.

"So he made it a sort of rule, you see, that all the future owners of this castle should have at least one deerhound as a protector. It was kept to faithfully. Generations of Skelton Castle's owners have kept a deerhound, or more, on the property, and in each group there has been one named Aminta, after the brave dog that saved Sir Hector."

"How wonderful," Mandy said. "That explains the graveyard we found."

"Ah, yes." Mrs. Noble sighed. "We try to take care of it, from time to time. But with our old bones it isn't easy now."

"Well," Tom Noble went on, getting into his stride, "Miss Amelia Skelton's own Aminta was the light of her life. The two were inseparable. Then, one night, Miss Skelton called Molly and me to her bedside."

"Oh, it was a shame to see her so upset," Molly Noble remembered. "She was the last surviving member of the generations of Skeltons, you see — and she was terribly troubled by the fact that when they were gone, not only would there be no Skelton to run the castle, but no deerhound to protect it from an uncertain future."

"She had come up with a plan for making sure that a deerhound survived her to stay here," Tom Noble told them. "So Aminta was sent away for a while, and when she came back she was carrying a litter of pups."

"How brave she was, poor Miss Amelia," sniffed Mrs. Noble, lost in sad memories of Miss Skelton's last days. "She had clung to life, frail as she was, waiting desperately for the day when Aminta's puppies would be born, so she could die in peace."

"Did Aminta succeed in time?" Tilly asked, her eyes wide.

"Just one single female pup was born," Tom Noble said. "The other little ones were sickly and too weak to survive."

"She was overjoyed when Tom took the tiny puppy in to her. She held it to her cheek and kissed it. 'Aminta,' she said to the puppy, 'make sure Skelton Castle falls into the right hands when I'm gone.' And with that, her mission completed, she closed her eyes and was gone." Molly Noble wiped her nose with a lace handkerchief.

Mandy's eyes stung with tears. "What a sad story! I expect the puppy died, too, did it?" She could hardly bear to hear the answer to this question.

"No," Tom Noble said, softly. "It did not. Miss Skelton gave Molly and me this cottage as a gift so that we could live out our days here in peace. She gave us the puppy, too."

There was brief silence in the room. "But . . ." said Mandy, "I thought . . ."

"I thought you said the puppy was to be the future protector of Skelton Castle," James said, puzzled.

"Yes, we did. But only if they were the kind of people

who were worthy of carrying on the tradition, if you get my meaning."

"Worthy?" Tilly said.

"Miss Skelton made us promise that we would not hand over little Aminta to just *anybody* who took over the castle. We were, she said, to wait until we were certain that Aminta would be valued and respected by people who loved and respected the castle, too — and its great history," Molly Noble said firmly.

"What happened to Aminta — the mother dog?" Mandy asked. "She couldn't, by any chance, have . . . become lost?"

"Lost!" Mrs. Noble said. "Oh, no. She was adored around here. No, Aminta died, soon after her beloved mistress."

"Oh!" Mandy felt a stirring of sadness mixed with excitement. She asked: "What did Aminta look like? Did she have any unusual markings?"

"She had a marvelous white diamond in the middle of her chest," Tom Noble said. "An unusual mark that was distinctive."

Tilly gaped at Mandy, who gaped at James. Tilly coughed. "Are you . . . um . . . sure . . . Aminta is dead?"

"She died in my arms," Molly Noble told her. "Right here beside the hearth. She was a wonderful mother to her little pup, and fed her dutifully until she was old enough to eat solid food. Then it was as if the spark went out of her. She lost her energy, her will to live."

"She pined away," Tom Noble put in. "Dogs do die of broken hearts, you know. She went to be with Miss Skelton. That's where she belonged. At her mistress's side."

Nobody spoke. Mandy's thoughts were racing. Aminta *had* come to them, she knew it all along. Their Aminta was definitely the same dog that Mr. and Mrs. Noble had described. There was no longer any doubt in her mind.

"The puppy?" Mandy asked. "May we see it, please?"

Mr. and Mrs. Noble looked at each other.

"Well, now," Tom Noble began uncomfortably. "That all depends. You see, we've heard terrible things about the graveyard being sold off — about modern houses being put up, with security gates and guards, and about the Skelton land being divided for profit."

"We're very unhappy about it," Molly Noble said apologetically. "We don't feel that, with all this going on, the castle is a suitable place for little Aminta."

"But you don't understand," cried Tilly, leaping out of the chair. "My grandfather didn't divide the land to sell it. He only bought the piece that was left to buy. And he's going to have it stopped. He's been trying to get ahold of his lawyer to tell him not to allow the demolition to go ahead."

Molly and Tom Noble looked hard at each other. "Is this the truth?" Tom Noble asked, frowning.

"Absolutely," James cried. "Tilly's grandfather is committed to keeping the cemetery, now that he knows it's there and how historically important it is."

"Tilly and Mr. Blaithwaite have only been in the castle for a few days," said Mandy, "but in that short time we've learned the importance of saving this cemetery. You must trust us, Mr. and Mrs. Noble. Please. We're on your side."

"Your grandfather will get the demolition work stopped?" Mr. Noble asked. "The land will never be divided, nor the castle knocked down, nor the grounds ripped up?"

"Cross my heart," Tilly said solemnly.

"No fences?" Molly Noble said.

"Not a yard of it, anywhere," Tilly said.

Molly Noble smiled with relief. "Well, in that case," she said, "I'll go and wake Aminta — just for you to see. Agreed, Tom, dear?"

"Of course, Molly," Tom Noble said. "You do that."

# *Ten*

Aminta was carried into the living room in Molly Noble's arms. She blinked, brown eyes hazy from sleep, and looked around in bewilderment at the collection of faces looking back at her. "Oh," Mandy said, "she's absolutely gorgeous." Set down on the carpet, the puppy's long, slender legs wobbled and she sat down abruptly, then yawned and tumbled onto her side, legs wiggling comically.

James laughed. "How old is she?"

"She's about two and a half months old now," Tom Noble told him. "She's been a good girl, too, since she lost her mom. She's quick to learn."

Aminta stood up and ran over to have a closer look at the visitors. She put her front paws on Tilly's knees and stretched up to smell her face. Mandy noticed that she had the same white diamond shape on her small chest. Her coat was darker, sleeker, and her tail was smooth rather than shaggy, but it was her adorable little face that stole Mandy's heart. Tilly gathered Aminta into her lap and planted a kiss on the top of her head, and Mandy went over to pet her silky ears, raised up high in excitement and folded over at the top, like an envelope.

"She's so cute!" Tilly said. "But how would you both feel about Aminta coming to live at the castle?"

"It's her rightful place," Tom Noble said gruffly. "We'll miss her, but that's the job she was bred for and that's where she's meant to be."

"You'll be welcome to visit any time," Tilly assured them.

Molly Noble suddenly looked at her watch. "You'd better all be getting back now. It's so late! Tom and I will contact your grandfather tomorrow with our decision. Will that be all right?" She scooped Aminta into her arms.

Mandy struggled to mask her disappointment and saw that Tilly did, too. She should have realized that there was no way they were going to be allowed to take little Aminta away with them tonight. It would be too

unsettling for the puppy, and Mr. and Mrs. Noble still seemed to need convincing that Max Blaithwaite's intentions for Skelton Castle were truly honorable.

Aminta strained in Molly Noble's arms, tilted her head and yapped as Tilly, Mandy, and James left the cottage. Mr. and Mrs. Noble stood and waved to them in the doorway, having insisted that James replace the batteries in the flashlight before they left.

"If you see that stray deerhound again," Tom Noble called, "let me know, will you?"

"We will," Tilly called, and nudged Mandy hard with her elbow. "Bye."

"Come in!" shouted Max Blaithwaite as Tilly banged on the door with her fist the following morning. "My goodness, child, you'll knock the door down!"

"Gramps!" said Tilly. "We've got to talk to you!" Tilly was still in her pajamas, having shaken a sleepy Mandy and James awake soon after eight o'clock. She hurried over to the desk behind which her grandfather was sitting, poring over some important-looking documents. Mandy and James hesitated at the door. "Come on in, my dears," Mr. Blaithwaite invited them. "Don't mind the mess. I'm getting it straightened out. Well, Tilly, what have you discovered this time?"

"Gramps," she began again, "you and I have a duty to

make sure that this castle of ours has an Aminta — without delay!"

"An Aminta!" said Mr. Blaithwaite, wrinkling up his nose in complete confusion. "What *do* you mean, my dear girl?"

"Remember Sir Hector Skelton's diaries?" Mandy prompted eagerly. "The deerhound that saved him from death? And the graveyard he set up in her honor? And his wish that all future owners of the castle continue the tradition of owning a deerhound as protector?"

"Ah, yes, yes. There's no need to concern yourselves about that now. I've been in touch with Nigel Holden, my lawyer, who has in turn been in touch with Peter Weeks, the property developer. In principle, the man is prepared to accept the sum of money I've offered him in return for the land."

"Oh, wow, Gramps! That's wonderful news!"

"I had the hardest time getting hold of Nigel Holden, who struggled to track down Mr. Weeks," Mr. Blaithwaite went on. "Seems Nigel had been vacationing abroad. But late last night, when you were all sound asleep in your beds, the call we were hoping for came through from Mr. Weeks. He's a charming man, and most obliging." He chuckled in a satisfied sort of way.

"Mr. Blaithwaite," Mandy said, "Tilly and James and I

have been following a trail of clues since Saturday night and the clues have led us to the most wonderful deerhound puppy — named Aminta — who belongs here, as the castle's protector!"

"Can we keep her, please?" Tilly pleaded, her elbows on her grandfather's desk, her face inches from his. She jabbered off the details of the previous night's adventure. Eventually she drew in a breath.

"Well, I've never been against having another dog, as you know, Tilly," Mr. Blaithwaite said, holding Tilly at bay with the palm of his hand. "Now that we have the room for one, I don't see why not. Dogs need plenty of space, I believe, and regular walking." Mr. Blaithwaite suddenly looked thoughtful. "Well, I must say, this is all very confusing. I think that what you are trying to tell me is that you believe the ghost of this pup's mother led you to her — is that it?"

"Yes," Tilly said, triumphantly. "That's exactly what happened. Aminta — the mother dog — also showed us that the backhoes are already in place for destroying the graveyard of her ancestors!"

"Well, they won't get any farther than where they are now. And I, for one," said Max Blaithwaite, "am certainly grateful to this mysterious Aminta for the part she played in rescuing poor Oscar."

Tilly slung an arm around her grandfather's shoulder. "Thanks, Gramps," she said. "Thanks for believing."

"Thanks for taking action!" James said.

"I'm sure Aminta will rest in peace, knowing that the graveyard is safe and that her puppy is here at Skelton Castle. You could call the puppy Minty, for short," Mandy suggested.

"Yes," said Tilly happily. "Minty — perfect!"

"Suppose Mr. and Mrs. Noble decide not to let you have her after all?" James said gloomily.

"They have to!" Tilly said. "We're capable, after all. Anyone can see that."

The old-fashioned telephone on Max Blaithwaite's desk rang loudly, making them all jump. Mr. Blaithwaite went to grab it. Tilly grabbed Mandy around the waist and danced with her excitedly. "I'm going to have a puppy! I'm going to have a puppy!" she chanted. James grinned at them. Then they heard Mr. Blaithwaite say:

"Good heavens! Really? Oh, it can't be so! Yes, of course, I'll do my best. Thank you."

"What?" Tilly and Mandy said together, when Mr. Blaithwaite had put down the telephone.

"Tilly, Mandy, James, you must quickly go to the site of this cemetery. At once! Mr. Weeks called from London. He is perfectly willing to put a stop to his digging, but has failed to contact his contractor — the man who is due to dig up the site. I had no idea it was to begin so soon." Mr. Blaithwaite wrung his hands.

"When?" Mandy whispered, horrified.

"This very morning. They might have started already." Tilly sprang for the door, shouting for James and Mandy to follow. "I'll get Booth to help me down there as soon as possible — urge the man to wait, for heaven's sake!"

But they didn't hear the end of Mr. Blaithwaite's sentence. Tilly was running through the halls of the castle, her feet slapping loudly on the stone floors. Mandy and James charged after her. *Don't let it be too late, please,* Mandy pleaded silently. *We can't let you down now, Aminta, we just can't!*

Tilly chose the route through the gardens of the castle, and Mandy guessed she would have dismissed the idea of taking the tunnel because she hadn't had time to get her flashlight. James soon passed Tilly and went racing ahead toward their goal. Mandy followed as fast as she could, but found it difficult to see clearly because her eyes kept filling with nervous tears.

"Hey!" yelled James, as he saw the mighty stones of the ancient cemetery wall up ahead. "Wait! Stop!" The ominous sound of the deep rumbling of a powerful engine could clearly be heard. Hearing James shout, Mandy angrily wiped away her tears and used every last bit of her energy to go faster. She was in time to see James fling himself around the corner of the wall, his sides heaving with his effort, then stumble and fall on his knees. Tilly was seconds behind James. The bulldozer, they saw, had been driven up to the gate of the graveyard.

They stood and gaped, panting. The engine had been started, but there was no sign of the driver — in or out of the machine. They looked around. "Nobody's here," James gasped.

"Someone must be here. The machine's going," Mandy gasped.

"Hey! Is somebody out there?" The furious shout

came from within the cemetery itself. James, Tilly, and Mandy hurried along the wall to the gate where the ivy had been hacked away. Although they had left the gate open when they had come through the previous evening, it was now closed, though not padlocked. Behind the black, wrought-iron bars of the gate, the red and perspiring face of a stocky, angry man could be seen. He peered through the bars, his fists clenched by his side.

"Troublemakers!" he spat. "You call off your dog, do you hear me? I've been held a prisoner in here for an hour or more. Get the brute locked up so I can get on with my work!"

"Dog?" said Tilly, looking up and down the outer wall of the graveyard.

"We don't have a dog, except Blackie, and he's in the kitchen with Mrs. Booth having his breakfast," Mandy said, her heart pumping with joy. *Good old Aminta*, she cheered silently.

"Are you sure," James said mischievously, "that you didn't just *imagine* a dog?"

"I've got work to do!" screamed the man. "That dog has been snarling at me through this gate! I switched on the backhoe, then came in here to look around, and the beast wouldn't let me out again! What a waste of good diesel. My cell phone's been ringing its head off in the car, and I haven't been able to get out to answer it!"

Tilly, Mandy, and James grinned happily at one other.

"It's just as well," Tilly said. "Because the work here has been canceled — by Mr. Weeks, your boss in London."

"What?" The man snatched his hat off his head and flung it to the ground in irritation.

"That's what we came to tell you," Mandy said sweetly. "Mr. Weeks is not having the site cleared anymore, thank you."

"Stand aside," he bellowed. Tilly opened the gate and they made way for him to pass. The man put one foot outside the gate and looked warily up and down for the sign of a dog. "It was a big, hairy, gray thing, with its teeth bared," he mumbled, "like something out of a horror film." He picked up his hat.

"Hello!"

The man, who was wiping his forehead with his hat, turned. Max Blaithwaite was limping along toward them, Booth holding his arm. "My dear fellow! What an inconvenience we've put you through. It's all changed, you see. We're keeping the land intact. I'm glad we caught you in time. I'm Max Blaithwaite, the castle owner." He put out his hand.

"I won't bother, thank you, sir. I've had a bad start to the day and I'll just take my backhoe now and leave, if you don't mind. You should lock up that awful dog of yours, sir, if you don't mind my saying."

Max Blaithwaite's hand fell limply to his side. He frowned in bewilderment as the man climbed into the backhoe. "Dog?" he said. "What dog?"

Mandy, Tilly, and James burst out laughing. It was with a sense of real triumph that they watched the backhoe being driven away.

"Well," said Mr. Blaithwaite. "There is no accounting for some people's manners, right, Booth? A cold drink is what we all —"

He was interrupted by the sound of excited yapping. A soft gray bundle of fur on very long legs was loping toward them across the grass. Her ears flew behind her and her pink tongue hung out.

"Minty!" shouted Mandy in delight.

"Minty!" cried James and Tilly. The puppy bounced and jumped around in an ecstasy of excitement, trying to lick the many hands that reached out to her simultaneously.

"Gramps," said Tilly. "This is Minty, the puppy we were telling you about."

"She's wonderful! But will she get along with Oscar?" Max Blaithwaite said wearily.

Tom and Molly Noble were standing shyly a few

yards away. In Molly's hand was a bunch of pale pink rosebuds. Tom spoke up, "She's a good girl, sir," he said. "She'll do as she's told."

"Can we keep her then? Mr. and Mrs. Noble? Gramps?" Tilly burst out with enthusiasm.

"She'd be very welcome, Tilly," said Max Blaithwaite.

"We saw the bulldozer driving away," said Molly Noble happily. "We're so relieved. And of course you can keep her."

When Mrs. Noble had left her roses on Aminta's grave, she and her husband were persuaded to come back to the castle with Minty to settle her in. They walked slowly, keeping to Max Blaithwaite's gentle pace, enjoying the sight of Minty tumbling through the undergrowth. *The garden*, Mandy thought, *is going to be a perfect playground for little Minty.*

They came across Mandy's parents, trudging back up the hill from the yard with Jack Stone. Blackie was with them. Seeing the bigger dog, Minty lay down on her tummy and rolled over onto her back, allowing Blackie to sniff her all over. Blackie's tail wagged a welcome, and Minty got up again to play. "Mom! Dad!" Mandy shouted and ran to them. "We've had the most wonderful time."

"Hello, everyone," said Dr. Adam cheerfully. "Goodness, Mandy, you look as if you haven't been to sleep since we last saw you!"

"I'm sorry we weren't around to welcome you back," Mr. Blaithwaite said. "We were forced to quickly go solve a problem we had."

"Don't worry about that. We know our way around. We went to see Oscar, who's looking much happier." Dr. Emily laughed. "But who is *this*?" Minty put her front paws on Dr. Emily's knees and wagged her tail. "You've gotten a puppy in the time we've been away?"

"This is Minty — and it's a long story!" Tilly laughed.

Mr. Blaithwaite introduced Mr. and Mrs. Noble to Dr. Emily, Dr. Adam, and Jack Stone. "Ah, you're the people who live in the cottage down the road," Jack said. "I've been curious about the place. You've got a fine vegetable patch there, Mr. Noble."

"I can't seem to do much with it these days, son," Tom Noble said. "It needs younger muscles to do it justice."

"Anytime you need a hand, you call on me, Mr. Noble," Jack said. "I love gardening — and vegetable gardening especially."

"I will, thank you." Tom Noble smiled.

"And you'll both always be most welcome at Skelton Castle," Max Blaithwaite assured Mr. and Mrs. Noble. "You must come up and visit little Minty, of course."

They made their way to the kitchen, where Ellie Booth had put out a lavish lunch. Minty swirled around her pink legs, darting a happy tongue out for a lick and making Mrs. Booth shriek and giggle. "Hello there, sweetie. I bet you want a bowl of something cool, right?"

Then Booth appeared in the door, a polishing cloth in his hand. Scowling glumly, he made an announcement. "There's something strange going on in this castle, Mr. Blaithwaite," he began, shaking his finger. "Ever since we came, there has been a large, red velvet cushion lying at the foot of the bed in old Miss Amelia Skelton's bedroom. Well, I was in there cleaning today — and it's gone! There's no trace of it. Miss Tilly, have you or either of your friends been in there and taken it?"

Tilly solemnly shook her head. "No, Booth. I've never seen it." But Tilly looked at Mandy and James and gave them a big, happy wink. And Mandy thought, *Wonderful, courageous Aminta.* She wouldn't be back to howl in the night in the dungeon of Skelton Castle, but wherever she was now, she was comfortable, and at peace.